PLAYED BY HIM

NEW PLEASURES BOOK 2

M. S. PARKER

BELMONTE PUBLISHING, LLC

READING ORDER

Thank you so much for reading Played by Him, the second book in the New Pleasures series. If you'd like to read the complete series, I recommend reading them in this order:

1. Claimed by Him
2. Played by Him (This Book)
3. Saved by Him

ONE

THE SUNLIGHT GLEAMED OFF THE OCEAN. IMPOSSIBLY *blue water lapped at impossibly white sand. A cloudless sky and scorching sun was perfectly offset by a sea-salt-scented breeze. The perfect combination of heat and sun and wind.*

A spicy scent surrounded me as he ran his hands over my sweat-slicked skin. Up my back and then down, over my ass and down my legs. His thumbs worked into knotted muscles, then spread my cheeks.

A hot, wet tongue probed at my pussy, and I moaned, pushing back for more. Little trickles of pleasure rippled across my nerves, and I wanted it to never end. This place. This feeling. Being here with him. I wanted to stay here and never have to go back to the real world.

But the real world was calling...

Awareness came to me in stages.

I was inside, and the little bit of light coming between the curtains was fairly gray.

I was on a bed with nice sheets. Really nice sheets. That smelled amazing.

As did the body above me. Spicy. Like the sunscreen from my dream.

Heat radiated off him, caressing my skin. His hands were on me too. Palms skimming and fingers massaging. Part of my dream made reality.

I moaned, and he chuckled, the sound as sensual as silk whispering across skin.

"Good morning." His voice was rough as he leaned down and pressed a kiss to the top of my spine.

"I was having an amazing dream," I said, my own voice thick with sleep.

"Were you?" He massaged up the backs of my thighs, his thumbs brushing the bottom of my cheeks. "Better than this?"

I looked over my shoulder at him. "A little."

He raised an eyebrow, humor dancing in his amazing turquoise eyes. "How so?"

I flushed but didn't hesitate to share. "You had your mouth on me."

"Let me remedy that." He pushed my legs apart and settled between them, his wide shoulders tucking under my thighs as he pulled up my hips, and then his mouth was on me.

Jalen Larsen was a gorgeous twenty-seven-year-old billionaire tech genius, but at the moment, all I could think about was that he had an insanely talented tongue.

It danced around, drawing patterns on sensitive flesh, each one sending a ripple of pleasure through me that made what I'd felt in the dream pale by comparison. I closed my eyes and let my head fall down to the mattress. I didn't let myself think of the mechanics, instead focusing on the sensations coursing through me. Letting myself *feel* rather than *think*.

I squirmed, my nipples rubbing pleasantly against the sheets, and he chuckled again, this time sending vibrations through me. A moment later, a finger slid inside me.

"Mmm..." I made a pleased sound.

"Fuck, babe, you're so wet."

When he shifted positions, I sucked in a breath. His tongue was venturing somewhere new. He'd told me once that he'd do this, but I hadn't really expected it like this.

"Relax, Rona." He added a second finger in my pussy, twisting them even as he moved them in and out of me. "I'm not planning on fucking your ass just yet. Just enjoy yourself."

I opened my mouth to give a smart reply but ended up only swearing when his tongue teased over my asshole. It felt strange, but not in a bad way. I liked it, in fact.

It shouldn't have surprised me that he knew what I'd like even when I didn't. He'd understood me almost from the first moment we'd touched. What we had between us wasn't 'normal,' but it was...strong. This connection, it was something I couldn't explain, but I couldn't deny it either. He made me feel things...

He sank his teeth into my ass cheek, and I yelped.

"Stop thinking."

Thinking was almost always a problem for me. I had so much going on in my head that I sometimes lost sight of who I was. Of what was important. What was good in my life.

We were home. Safe. My father was back in prison where he belonged. Justice had won. Clay and I were friends. Jalen and I had dealt with our issues. I was still mourning Adare, but I understood grief, and I knew she would've understood me letting it go for this.

His fingers moved inside me, finding that spot that made me forget everything except the current of electricity it sent rushing across my nerves until I shattered. As I came, he pulled his fingers out, and I whimpered, my body convulsing again as a mini-orgasm rolled through me.

He pulled my hips up until I was on my knees, but when I tried to lift myself onto my hands, my arms wouldn't hold me. He chuckled as I slumped onto my elbows, bracing myself for what I knew was coming. A moment later, he drove into me, and I cried out as my body stretched too fast.

He froze for a moment. "Are you–"

"Don't stop." I barely managed to get the words out. "Please, fuck, don't stop."

"Your wish is my command."

I could hear the grin, and it made me smile too. I'd smiled during sex before, but this was different. This was humor. I'd had heat and friendship during the few weeks that Clay Kurth and I had been in our 'friends with bene-fits' stage, but I'd never had actual humor during sex.

I liked it. Almost as much as I liked the way Jalen felt inside me. *Almost*...because there was absolutely nothing that could compare to the way we fit together, the thickness and length of him, how much my body molded itself to accommodate him. As if nothing as small as spatial relations could keep us from being as physically close as two people could be.

"You're doing it again," he said as he slammed into me hard enough to jar my thoughts. "No thinking."

My retort came out breathless. "I thought I was in charge."

He leaned over me and put his lips at my ear. "Now, what made you think that?"

He laughed again, and there was heat in the sound. The sort of heat that sent the flames inside me roaring, consuming me from the inside out. I was going to come again, this time with fire rather than lightning. He reached down and wrapped his fingers around my wrists. As he pulled my arms behind my back, I knew I could resist him and he'd let go, but I didn't even consider it. I might have teased about being in charge, but I liked the freedom that came with not being in control.

My cheek rested on the bedspread as my hands settled at the small of my back, the position somewhat awkward but not necessarily uncomfortable. I had a feeling, though, that my neck and shoulders would complain if I was left this way too long. He used one hand to hold my wrists in place while the other moved to my hip.

"Good?" he asked.

I nodded as best I could. "Good."

He didn't attempt to ease me into anything, trusting that I would tell him if I couldn't take it. The next thrust took my breath away, and what came after kept me gasping for air, each inhalation driven out of me by the snap of his hips, the angle of penetration, the ache in my shoulders. Overwhelming contradictory sensations converged into one tight knot low in my belly, a white-hot explosive just waiting to blow my world apart.

"Fuck, J," I panted. "Don't stop. So good. So good. Don't stop. Fuck. Please. Just like that."

His thumb slid down my crease, stopped, pushed.

I came with a wordless scream.

He kept going, cursing as I convulsed around him. His thumb popped out, but I barely noticed. Each stroke sent another orgasm rolling over me. Or maybe they kept that first one going. I didn't know, and it didn't matter. His grip on my wrists tightened, and he pulled me upright, my back against his front. He wrapped his arm around my waist, driving up into me.

"Close," he grunted, "so close."

"Fucking hot." I let my head fall back on his shoulder. "Fucking hot when you come. Should be fucking illegal."

He pressed his lips to the top of my head. I turned toward him so he could take my mouth. His tongue twisted with mine in a scorching kiss. His hips jerked, losing his rhythm. The kiss became sloppy, desperate as he chased his release. I reached up, burying my fingers in his hair, the rich brown strands as soft as they looked. He bit my bottom lip, and I groaned into his mouth. A shudder passed through him, and his cock twitched, then pulsed as he came.

We collapsed onto the bed, a pile of sweaty, trembling limbs. Soon, we'd need to get up, return to the real world.

We had jobs and friends and family, bills to pay and responsibilities to care for, lives that we'd put on hold.

But right now, in this moment, I could just lay here and exist. Me and him and nothing else, no one else. He was my respite, and I intended to appreciate every second we had together.

TWO

I STUDIED MY REFLECTION IN THE MIRROR, A STRANGE feeling of self-consciousness attached to the happiness I'd been feeling ever since we arrived back in Fort Collins, Colorado. It wasn't really about my appearance. I was used to being self-conscious about that, wondering if my scar was showing, if the shirt I was wearing was long enough to cover everything when I moved, if the neck was high enough.

Now, when I looked in the mirror and saw the familiar ash blonde hair and china-blue eyes, I wondered if people saw beyond that, if they could see the way I felt. Even though I knew it was silly, I felt like I should be glowing or something.

I'd had moments of happiness with Clay as a friend and as a lover. Moments with Uncle Anton where I'd forgotten that I should have had a different path. My life since my mother's death hadn't been all doom and gloom, but it hadn't been like this either. It wasn't about perfect circumstances or not being sad over Adare's death. It was about letting myself see a positive future, and with Jalen, with this life I had begun to build here, I could see it.

I turned away from the mirror and headed back into the office. I'd spent the last couple hours organizing and sorting through things. It had been less than two weeks since Adare's death, and I hadn't exactly taken the time to go through her possessions. Even when she was dying, she'd kept up with the bills, with the clients, and when I found the envelope with my name on it, I knew why.

I walked back over to the desk and sat in the chair. The envelope sat on the gleaming wood, and I stared at it, trying to work up the courage to open it.

This was how I knew I was really happy. Even the grief at losing Adare wasn't the sharp, debilitating agony that I'd known in the past. I missed her, and that wouldn't go away anytime soon, but I'd known her well enough to know that she wanted me to be happy.

I let out a slow breath, picked up the envelope, and opened it.

Rona,

I'm guessing, right now, you're pretty pissed at me for not telling you I was sick. I'm sorry about that. I'm sure we had this discussion at some point, and this letter isn't to go over it all again. It's to reassure you that you can do this. I wouldn't have left Burkart Investigations to you if I didn't have faith that you could make it into everything I always wanted it to be. Don't doubt yourself.

I'm getting close to the end now, and now I'll ask you to

forgive me for taking liberties that I might not have yet earned.

I know there are things in your past that you don't want to share, and I respect your privacy. I haven't gone snooping. I like to think that if we had more time together, you would have eventually trusted me with some of those secrets, and maybe you would have taken some advice. Since we didn't have that time, I'll ask for some leeway when it comes to telling you something I wish I would have figured out when I was your age.

Don't be afraid to live the life you've always wanted.

It doesn't matter if that life is being single and running a private investigation firm, or getting married and being a stay-at-home mom. Go back to college or become an apprentice. Make friends or be a loner. Find a man, a woman, or both. The opportunities are endless.

Don't allow fear of your past, or of your future, to keep you from reaching that potential.

I swallowed hard, a painful lump in my throat.

Now, for a few final things.

Don't let Wendy Mikelson weasel her way out of payments. She knows that she doesn't get a frequent customer discount. If she has a problem paying the bill, remind her that she can always ask her son to tell her where he's going at all times rather than having us follow him.

Don't take any cases from Hiram Whitehouse. He believes that aliens impregnate his chickens every few months. He's harmless, and I don't like taking money from him for his flights of fancy, so I just suggest he take any suspicious eggs to his vet. Orville knows all about the alien chickens and doesn't mind turning them into omelets.

When the bathroom sink gets plugged up, before you call a plumber, use the wrench in the toolbox to take off the bottom pipe. It'll save you sixty bucks even if it makes you curse.

Go to at least one Rams game and mingle with the locals. Become a part of the community, even if you're an introverted one.

And, finally, I believe in you, kid. I'm just sorry I won't be around to see everything you're going to accomplish.

Love, Adare

I set the letter back on the desk and rubbed the backs of my hands across my cheeks. I'd always known that life wasn't fair – when your father murdered your mother and two other people and left you literally scarred for life, the world being *unfair* was sort of a given – but thinking about how my father was still alive while Adare was dead really drove the point home.

I'd wanted to become an FBI agent to make a difference, to protect people the way I hadn't been able to protect my mother. When I'd gotten kicked out of the academy for lying about changing my name and about my father's murder conviction, I'd felt like I'd failed my mother. Becoming a PI hadn't been part of the plan at all. Then the case Jalen had brought me ended up leading to the arrests of several human traffickers and the rescue of several teenage girls. *That* had made a difference.

Maybe I could make my mother proud *and* do what Adare had asked of me and run Burkart Investigations. I'd probably still have to take cases like lost pets or following possibly cheating spouses, but I could find other cases too.

In fact, I realized with pure clarity, I already knew someone who worked important cases with the FBI even though she wasn't an agent. Jenna Archer. The victim of a childhood horrific enough to make my family look like the Bradys, Jenna was a computer genius, and she'd helped FBI agent Raymond Matthews take down several human trafficking and child pornography rings. Oddly enough, Agent Matthews was Clay's partner, both of them working out of the Denver office.

All these pieces of my life had come together in a way that I'd never expected, never could have predicted. If I was someone who believed in destiny or fate, I might've thought that was what was happening here, but I'd seen too much shit to want to believe that there was some higher power or higher reason making things happen.

I preferred to think that the accident that had turned my loving father into a murderous monster had been just that. A series of circumstances and events, results of choices or complete happenstance. Why would I want to believe that there had been a reason for my mother being brutally murdered? For Jenna being pimped out by her own mother? For my uncle being shot to death?

I shook my head. Too many maudlin thoughts. I'd come here happier than I'd been since I was a kid, and I wanted that back.

Work. That's what I needed to focus on. Get back to the entire reason I'd come here to begin with. Keeping my promise to Adare.

Even though we'd – *I'd* – been closed for two weeks, I did have a case to work on while I waited for others to come in.

I'd met Jenna on a case. She hired me to find the half-brothers and sisters her mother had given up or had taken from her. I'd gathered some information about them already, but between Adare's hospitalization and death, and then my needing to go back to Indiana for my father's new trial, things had been on hold. Now, it was time to pick them back up again.

Fortunately, my whiteboard was still against the far wall, turned around to prevent clients from seeing personal information, and everything I'd put on it before was still there.

I walked across the office and turned the board so I could refresh my memory. At the top was Jenna's mother. I'd listed all of the aliases I'd been able to find, including what I knew of which name Jenna's mother used for the different births, and the approximate years each child was born. I still had a lot of blanks to fill, and I intended to work my ass off to give Jenna a chance to know siblings who might end up being a part of her life.

I'd focus on the kids who were born after Helen Kingston's arrest and induction into Witness Protection, mostly because that was the research I could do around here. In another one of those strange twists that I kept seeing, Helen had been sent from Florida to Cheyenne, Wyoming...where she ended up being far too close to Jenna. It was a fuck up of epic proportions on the part of the US Marshals. One that had almost gotten Jenna killed a few years ago.

But, there was one positive to her having been that close. If – no, *when* – I found her siblings, they'd be close enough for them to have a relationship if they wanted it. The older ones would be more difficult to locate, but if there was a way to find them, I'd do it.

I couldn't change what Jenna had been through, but I could do this for her.

THREE

JUST TO LOOK AT JALEN, I WOULDN'T KNOW HOW MUCH money he had. Even when he was in a suit or tux rather than his customary casual shirt and jeans, he still looked like he didn't quite fit in with the caviar crowd. Then I pulled up to his house, and it was obvious that there was more to him than a handsome face.

Maybe it was a good thing that Jalen had already met Clay. I didn't have anyone else I considered family, which meant there was none of the usual anxiety when it came to doing the whole 'meet the parents' thing. I couldn't imagine what it would've been like if I had to figure out the best time to tell my parents I was dating a billionaire.

Dating.

Was that what Jalen and I were doing?

Our history was short and...odd. We met when he'd come to hire me for a case, and he'd argued with me when I'd gotten hurt working that same case. The argument had turned into a kiss which had turned into hot sex right there in the office. Things hadn't gone smoothly from there, but after he'd been there for me during my father's trial, we'd decided to see where things went between us.

We just hadn't given it a name. Or a label. Which meant I was either walking toward the front door of my boyfriend's house...or I'd dressed up for dinner and a booty call.

The biggest problem was, I didn't know which of those options I wanted.

"Hey," he said as he opened the door. He was smiling, but I could see hints of strain in his eyes, the way he fidgeted with the side of his pants.

"Hey." I leaned in and kissed his cheek.

At least, I tried to kiss his cheek. What ended up happening was that he tried to do the same thing, and I ended up catching his chin while he kissed the tip of my nose. That awkwardness, combined with being nervous, made me burst out laughing. A second later, Jalen did the same, and just like that, the tension between us evaporated.

"This is weird, isn't it?" he said as he led me into the kitchen. "I don't mean in a bad way."

"No, I get it," I said. "We've sort of done things backward, and with all of the crazy shit that's been going on, we haven't had a chance to do anything normal like...well, like the dinner that smells absolutely amazing."

"I hope it does." He gave me that charming grin of his. "I slaved away in a hot kitchen all day."

I laughed again. "I guess that means I should set the table then, since you worked so hard on the – what are we having again?"

"Stuffed-cheese pasta, Italian bread, and a fruit salad." He went over to the oven and peeked inside. "And choco-late-covered strawberries for dessert."

I breathed in deeply. "That all sounds amazing." With a smile, I started looking through the cabinets for dishes.

A nice, normal date with my...boyfriend? Lover? Friend?

Well, whoever he was to me, I was certain of at least one thing. If the food tasted as great as it smelled, I would keep him around for just that.

THIS WAS...DIFFERENT.

We'd eaten dinner – and it had tasted as wonderful as it'd smelled – and then Jalen asked if I wanted to watch a movie. That was how I ended up on his couch, tucked up against his side, his arm around me, wondering what I should do now that Meg Ryan and Tom Hanks had found their happily ever after. I'd never done the whole dinner and movie thing with anyone except a group, and even then, it hadn't been often. There'd been no expectations, no feelings to consider.

I was beginning to remember why I didn't really do the whole dating thing.

Jalen shifted first. Not a lot, but enough to tell me that he was going to initiate whatever came next. Judging by the way things between us had gone from moment one, I would've been surprised if he suggested we end the night here.

He didn't.

He hooked a finger under my chin, raising my head until we were looking right at each other. He'd dimmed the lights for the movie, but the lighting did little to hide the desire on his face. His thumb brushed across my bottom lip, sending a zing of electricity through those cells.

I stretched up to meet him as he lowered his head. The kiss started off gentle, lips leisurely moving together, a hint of tongue sliding across sensitive skin. As much as I knew he wanted me, there was none of the desperation that had characterized most of our previous encounters. Without the need to rush, we had the time to explore each other's bodies, learn the subtler ways of turning each other on. I ran my hands over his broad shoulders and down his muscular arms. The man's body was a work of art. I doubted I'd ever get tired of seeing him, touching him.

I'd never had this before, the freedom of being completely bared to a man's eyes, his hands, not even with Clay. Jalen was the only man who'd ever seen me without a shirt. Well, sort of. After everything about my dad came out, I'd shown Clay my scar, but we hadn't been sleeping together at that point, and it hadn't been a part of anything sexual, so it was still different.

When Jalen lowered the side zipper to my dress, it was everything sexual. Without interrupting our kiss, I helped him remove my dress, leaving me in my favorite bra and panty set. Sexy, but not so much so that they weren't functional.

His hands moved across my skin, fingers tracing my scar

from where it ended at my spine around my right side. As his tongue breached my mouth, one hand pushed under my bra to palm my breast. His fingers brushed against the space between my breasts where my scar started before moving to my nipple. He touched the scar tissue like it was any other part of my skin, and it made something deep in my chest ache.

I moaned into his mouth as he teased my nipple into a hard point, and I was suddenly aware that my bra was gone. I didn't think too long on it, preferring to focus on what he was doing with my breast. As he tugged on my nipple again, he rocked against me, his cock hard against my thigh. I dropped one hand between us, fondling him through his pants. His mouth broke away from mine as he hissed out a breath, squeezing his eyes closed.

"Damn, babe, you're going to make me embarrass myself."

The thought of being able to make him lose control made me wet – something I filed away to try later – but that wasn't what I wanted tonight. I wanted him inside me when he finally came. Still, I couldn't stop myself from teasing him.

"I thought you had more control than that."

His eyes darkened, and he grabbed me around my waist, turning us so that I was stretched out beneath him on the couch. He balanced on one arm as he moved the other between us. His gaze locked on mine, and I found myself barely able to breathe. He slid his fingers beneath the waistband of my panties, moving over the thin layer of pale curls to what was hidden beneath.

"Should we put your control to the test?" he asked as he slid a single finger between my folds. "Don't come."

I squirmed as he teased me, the tip of his finger gliding back and forth across my clit. He didn't need to worry about me coming. His touch was too light, not offering the friction I needed if I was going to get off. Then his hand moved lower, his palm pressing down on my clit as his finger slid inside of me.

"Don't come," he warned again.

His hand moved back and forth, slowly at first, then faster. A second finger joined the first, and he pressed down harder, putting almost painful pressure on my clit, but I didn't ask him to let up. I couldn't have formed the words if I'd tried. I writhed under his touch, nails scrabbling against the couch as I tried to fight off my climax.

"I can't," I finally gasped. "I have to come. I have to. I can't stop. Please."

"Don't," he said, his voice firm. "Don't come until I say you can."

I arched my back, teeth sinking into my bottom lip as I tried to think of something, anything, that could keep me from tipping over the edge. Any thought I tried to focus on vanished before I could get ahold of it, the sensations rippling through my body too powerful for me to ignore. I was going to come, and there was nothing I could do to stop it.

Suddenly, his hand was gone, and I dropped back to the couch, staring up at him with wide, hazy eyes. Blood rushed in my ears, and my heart pounded against my ribs.

My entire body was humming with electricity, overheated with no relief in sight.

"J," I growled, grabbing at his shirt.

He gave me that obnoxiously cocky grin of his, pushing himself up to take off his shirt. He didn't bother removing his pants, only undoing them enough that he could free his cock, and then he was settling between my legs again.

"You can come now," he said.

I opened my mouth to say something snarky and possibly intelligent, but only a scream made it out as he buried himself inside me. My entire body seized up as I climaxed, and I could do nothing but ride it out as Jalen pounded into me, rolling one orgasm into another until everything started to go dark. I heard him groan my name, and then, nothing.

FOUR

SCREAMING. THEY WERE SCREAMING. WHY WASN'T *anyone helping them? Someone needed to help them.*

I couldn't do it. I couldn't get up. I couldn't even feel my own body.

Then I could feel it, and I wished I couldn't.

That's when I realized that I was the one who was screaming.

Screaming about how much I hurt. Screaming for help. Screaming for someone to stop him.

Stop him.

He was going to kill her.

Stab her. Leave her bleeding.

No. He'd already done that. He'd killed her, and I'd seen her.

Wait, not her. Her.

I watched as he grabbed her hair when she tried to run. He yanked her back, and her feet slipped in all that blood.

She started to scream, and his blade moved across her throat, opening flesh and spilling blood.

The heavy scent and taste of iron and copper flooded my nose, my mouth. It coated my tongue, and I gagged. A fresh wave of pain tore through me.

I screamed...

And jerked awake.

My hand went to my chest automatically, then to my side. I sat up and caught my breath as a burning pain shot down my spine and then the back of my leg.

"Fuck." I forced myself to swing my legs over the side of the bed and stood, grimacing at the pain.

I raised my arms over my head, then twisted, bent, stretching out the tight muscles in my back and side. As I moved, the pain didn't fade, but I knew it would take time. When my father had cut me from sternum to spine, he'd miraculously missed major organs, but my nerves and muscles hadn't completely healed, at least not back to the way they were originally. Every couple months or so, I'd get a muscle spasm that would pinch a nerve, and this would happen.

Sometimes, it was almost like a memory of the pain I'd been in that day, a ghost. And it wasn't the only ghost that hovered around my subconscious, as my nightmare had reminded me.

Not that I'd ever really forgotten.

My hand automatically went to my chest. Like Jenna, I wore some of my reminders on my skin.

I limped into the bathroom and turned on the light. I would have to take things slow today, at least until my muscles relaxed and my nerves calmed down. It was a good thing Jalen and I hadn't made plans for tonight, because the way I was feeling right now, I doubted I could've handled another night like last night.

I smiled through the pain as I showered, letting the hot water ease my muscles. Sex with Jalen was like an athletic event. I'd been less sore after various FBI training exercises.

I needed to stop thinking about sex with Jalen, or I'd never get any work done. I picked up my bottle of shampoo. Then again, I did have some time now to think things over…

───

I WAS ALREADY FEELING BETTER by the time I got out of the shower. I dressed and headed to the kitchen to find a quick breakfast. Since it was down to only me, Burkart Investigations would be open only while I was there. I could be late without getting in trouble, but I could also possibly lose business if I didn't open on time.

I'd just washed my breakfast dishes and left them in the rack to dry when it hit me that I should probably hire someone to answer the phone and take down appointments when I wasn't there. It was either that, or whenever I was working a case that required me to actually leave the office, I'd have to lock up. Somehow, I didn't think that would be the best way to run a business.

My phone rang as I reached for the door. "Hello?"

"Are you back in Colorado?"

I blinked at the familiar voice. "Jenna?"

"Don't you look at your caller ID before you answer your phone?" I could hear the faint smile in her voice.

"Apparently not."

There was a moment of silence before she continued, more business-like now, "You didn't answer my question."

"Yes, I'm back in Colorado. I'm heading in to work right now, but once I get things settled, I'll call you and tell you how things went with Jalen."

"Just with Jalen?" she asked softly, and I could hear the compassion in her voice. "You don't want to tell me about the trial?"

I chuckled. "You're telling me that you weren't following it all week online?"

"I was. Congratulations."

I didn't know many people who'd have that as their response to a friend helping put her father back in prison. "I'll call you back in a little bit."

"I wasn't calling about Jalen."

I scowled as I stepped outside, but it had more to do with the gust of cold wind that nearly ripped the doorknob out of my hand than it did with Jenna staying on the phone. "Something else then?"

"Come by the house. I have something to discuss with you."

"I've been making a list of leads to follow on your case," I said as I dug for my keys.

"That's great, but I have a new case for you," she said, her voice growing grim, a bit strained. "That group of assholes you got arrested a couple weeks ago. Well, it looks like someone's taken over."

I stopped. "Taken over?"

"Yeah. Want to come by now?"

I didn't even need to think about it. "I'm on my way."

———

"LET me see if I understand this correctly," I said as I put my now-empty cup down on the table. "Less than a month after the Feds made tons of arrests, nothing's changed."

Jenna shrugged. "That's generally how these things go. Cut off one head, another one grows in its place."

"I thought that was seven more, not one."

She raised an eyebrow. "It's not Hydra."

I would've smiled at the comment, but I was too depressed over what she was telling me. "I can't believe that it didn't make any difference."

She leaned forward, her gray eyes intense. "It made a huge difference. You kept six girls from the sort of torture and abuse that you don't even want to think about." Shadows flickered across her face. "The time it's taken for someone else to get established here, you saved all of the kids they would've taken."

I ran my hand over my hair. "Is this how it always goes? Close one group down, but they never actually go away?"

Jenna leaned back in her chair. Her gaze fell on her arm, and she ran her fingers over the scar there. "If you listen to the cops or the FBI, they'll tell you that it's about keeping focused on the big picture, staying true to the course, all that sort of shit. But I can't look at it that way. I can't look at the big picture, or I'll go crazy."

She looked up at me, but her fingers still kept tracing the scar she had once told me came from a suicide attempt when she was only eight-years-old. The haunted look on her face made my stomach twist.

"I have to look at each life saved. Each person who will never have to go through what I went through. Each person who is rescued from that hell and given a chance at a better life. I know there are all these organizations that talk about eradicating slavery, but I don't know if that will ever be a possibility. I do know that I can save one person, two people, a group. And that's enough to keep me sane and working."

The moment hung heavy between us, and then she pushed back from the table and refilled our coffee.

"Anyway, I didn't bring you here just to tell you all of this," she said as she set down the mug again. "I wanted to know if you would like to help."

"Help?" I reached for the mug automatically, but I wasn't really even paying attention to it outside the warmth it would provide my cold fingers.

"I know you're working on my case, and you need to take other cases too," she said. "I'm not going to ask you to risk Adare's business. I just want to know how you'd feel about me possibly contacting you with some footwork for cases. I used to do all that myself, but with my kids..." She shrugged again.

I met her steady gaze. "I'd love to help out in any way I can. Just tell me what you want me to do."

FIVE

"Work's been keeping you busy," Jalen said as we headed into the city. "Does that mean things are going well?"

"They are." I twisted my fingers together as I glanced at him, then out the window. "I've been looking into Jenna's siblings, trying to get more information on the three kids I know were adopted out of Cheyenne, and I've been doing some legwork on a case against some human traffickers who are bringing people up from South America to work in sweatshops."

"Is that safe?" Jalen asked. He reached over and took my hand. "After what happened when you were looking for Meka–"

"I won't be talking to anymore high school kids." I threw him a smile. "Most of what Jenna has me doing is verification of things she's found online. Paper trails, that sort of thing. I get the impression that her methods aren't always...legal."

"Yeah, based on some conversations I've heard, that sounds about right," he said with a grin. "Jenna's brilliant."

"She is," I agreed. "I think that's one of the reasons why I want to make sure I don't let her down with the personal stuff. She could find her siblings, most of them at least, and help the FBI with their cases, all without me, but she's putting her family first, trying to keep things as legal as possible."

We pulled up in front of The Melting Pot, and neither one of us spoke until we were seated at the best table in the place. We'd had those moments of silence before, but this was different, I could feel it. This was our first real date. We'd done the dinner and movie thing, but that had been at his house. Jenna and Rylan knew we were a couple, but that was about all.

As far as the outside world was concerned, Jalen Larsen's bachelorhood was still intact.

This dinner of ours could change that. Fort Collins wasn't like New York or LA where paparazzi were all over the place, but if someone at the restaurant recognized Jalen as one of the city's celebrities and it was an otherwise slow news night, we could find pictures of ourselves in tomorrow's paper.

Neither one of us had talked about it, but I knew it had to be in the back of his head because it sure as hell had been in mine. We might not be referring to each other with the titles of boyfriend and girlfriend, but this couldn't be seen as anything other than a date.

After the wine had been poured and the waiter left,

Jalen sighed. "Does this feel as awkward to you as it does to me?"

I laughed, and the sound helped break some of that tension down. "You sound as if we haven't had a completely traditional relationship from moment one."

He laughed and took a drink of his wine. "That is an excellent point."

"We've had a rough few weeks," I said. "Let's talk about the stuff we haven't had a chance to talk about. Like, do you come here often?" As soon as the question was out of my mouth, heat flooded my face. "Shit. I can't believe I just asked that."

"It's a perfectly reasonable question." A smile played around his mouth. "And the answer is no. I don't come here very often. I've brought a few business contacts here, but no...dates."

He didn't have to say her name for me to know that he was specifically talking about his hopefully soon-to-be-ex-wife, model Elise Marx. They hadn't been together for a while, their prior attempt at a reconciliation destroyed when he caught her fucking a bodyguard. Now, she was holding up the divorce proceedings because she'd violated the terms of their prenuptial agreement and wanted a way around it. She was a real gem.

The waiter returned to take our orders, and I was glad for the distraction. When I'd asked if he'd come here before, I hadn't meant it to be a question about whether or not he'd brought Elise here, but I couldn't deny that I liked being the first one to have dinner with him here. A little nagging voice in the back of my head questioned the fact that this was usually his business restaurant, but I quickly shoved that away. No jumping to conclusions and no being petty. That was the only way this would ever work.

As the waiter walked away, I changed the subject. "Have you heard how Meka's doing?"

I hadn't seen the fifteen-year-old since finding her and five other girls held by men with guns. With Jalen's help, I'd gotten the police involved, and the girls had all been rescued, but between Adare's hospitalization and death, and my return to Indiana for a week, I hadn't taken the time to decide if I should visit Meka or not. After all, Jalen had been the one who'd hired me, and aside from a single interview with Meka's father, Theo, I didn't have a connection with the family.

"I talked with Theo a few days after the fact, and he said that she was doing well. A few scrapes and bruises, but no other physical harm. From what Meka told him about the other girls, it was the same for them."

I was sure the girls would be dealing with the repercussions of their kidnappings for a while, but it was still a relief to hear that none of them had been assaulted.

Jalen continued, "I guess what she went through really made her think about how fortunate she was to have a father like Theo and how it would devastate him if something happened to her. I'm sure they'll have some moments butting heads in the future, but from what he said, the rebellious attitude she's had since her mother died is gone."

"That's great." I blew out a relieved breath. "I'm glad something good came out of that terrible experience."

"You helped take down a human trafficking ring," he said. "I'd consider that pretty good."

My smile tightened. "It would be if another one wasn't already taking over."

Anger darkened his expression. "It never ends, does it?"

"Jenna says that she tries not to focus on the big picture, that she'd get too discouraged if she did. Instead, she thinks about each individual life that's been saved, as well as the ones who were never forced into slavery because of what she does." I toyed with the edge of my napkin. "I'm going to help her with the work she does for the FBI."

"Can I ask you a question? About the FBI?"

I'd been waiting for this to come back up. Jalen had sat through the trial and my testimony, which meant he knew everything about me. My real name, what my father had done, why I'd gotten kicked out of the FBI. Sometimes, having all the information only led to more questions, and I'd been wondering when he was going to start asking them.

"Go ahead."

"You had to know that you wouldn't be able to lie to them about the things that'd happened, but you tried anyway. Why'd you do it?"

"I wanted to help people," I said simply. "I have a degree in criminal justice from Columbia, and when Clay came to me my senior year and suggested I join, I thought I might as well try it. If I was going to get caught hiding my past, I figured why not do it with the FBI."

"You don't do anything by half-measures, do you?" he asked wryly.

"I don't see the point," I admitted. "But you're the same way. Graduated MIT with a doctorate at twenty-one. A millionaire by twenty-three after selling a business that came out of an app you created in college. And now you have Sylph Industries."

"You did your homework on me."

I shrugged. "It seemed like a good idea to know who I was getting into bed..." Heat flooded my cheeks. "I mean, business. Who I was getting into business with." I squirmed in my seat. "It was a good idea for bed too."

The corner of his mouth tipped up in a partial smile. "That reminds me. I still need your invoice for Meka's case."

"With everything that's been going on, I completely forgot." I dug my phone out of my purse. "I'll set a reminder right now."

"Are you going to try to manage Burkart Investigations on your own?" he asked.

"Adare had a receptionist for a while," I said, "but she worked the cases alone. I'm thinking about doing the same. Have someone at the office to answer calls and keep the calendar, but do the actual investigations myself."

"If I was working on something that could be used to find missing people, would you be willing to work as a consultant? Answering questions, pointing out flaws, that sort of thing."

"You want me to help you with an app?" I was flattered but wasn't entirely sure how much good I could be at something like that. I really hoped that he wasn't offering because he thought he needed to.

"I'm still in the brainstorming stage," he said. "Which is part of what I'd like your input about."

"Maybe you should tell me what you're trying to do first."

He flushed and gave me that self-deprecating grin I liked so much. "Sorry. Sometimes my mouth and my brain aren't in sync."

I flashed back to the other night when his mouth and brain were very much in sync, and a rush of heat flooded me. It took far more effort than I liked to bring my attention back to the present.

"I want to come up with ways to track people," he said, then hurried to clarify. "Not in a creepy way. I want something that's a combination of a GPS, so if a kid like Meka goes missing, there's a quick and efficient way of finding her, and a panic button. Even though Meka and her dad were having issues, when she realized what her boyfriend had done, I'm sure she would've used a panic button if she'd had one."

I let the idea turn over in my mind, looking at the possibilities – both negative and positive – as well as possible complications. I wasn't a tech person, which meant I didn't know how feasible the logistics were, but I could see some of the legal issues that would come up. I wasn't going to assume that's what Jalen wanted though.

"What, exactly, is it you want me to do?"

He leaned back as the waiter returned to clear away our appetizer plates and refill our wine. "Mostly, just let me pick your brain about problems we'd have, suggestions, recommendations, anything that you can think of that we might possibly need to know and answers to any questions I might come up with."

"Can I have some time to think about it?"

"Of course." He reached across the table and squeezed my hand. "I don't want you to do anything you aren't comfortable with." His thumb brushed across my knuckles. "And I don't want you to feel obligated. It's a sincere offer, but I don't want to risk what we have going here."

It was the perfect opening to ask him what that was, to get him to put into words this thing between us. But I couldn't bring myself to do it. I told myself that it was because I didn't want to sound like one of those women who want to know where things were going from moment one, but I knew that it was fear, plain and simple. I was terrified that he would tell me that what he felt wasn't the same as what I felt. That he wanted to keep things casual and we could both see other people.

I didn't want to see other people, and the thought of him with another woman made my stomach churn. In my head, I knew it'd be better to get it all out in the open, but logic wasn't ruling here. So, I smiled and turned the subject to our meal. We'd have a nice, uncomplicated date, and I'd figure out the rest later.

SIX

AFTER LOSING MY MOTHER IN INDIANA, AND MY uncle in New York, I didn't really miss either of the places I used to live. Now, I'd lost a friend here, but as much as I missed Adare, it wasn't the same as what happened before. Besides, I had other people I cared about in Fort Collins. Leaving wasn't something I was considering.

Still, as I walked across the cemetery, I couldn't help but feel that something was absent. Over the past couple months, I'd sometimes missed the trees that had surrounded me most of my life, but it was never more obvious than now. There were trees on the mountains, individuals or pairs scattered around, but so many were pines that it was still greener than the abundance of colors I'd been used to in the fall.

I'd never seen the place where my mom was buried, and Anton had been cremated, so I'd never really done the whole leaving flowers, spending time at the cemetery thing until now. Although I was new to this, as I approached

Adare's marker, I couldn't help but think that it looked far too bare. She'd paid for a simple headstone, and I'd gotten a letter a couple days ago that said it'd be installed this upcoming week.

"I should've brought flowers," I said softly as I stopped at the edge of the grave. "You always said you liked sunflowers."

I looked around. It was Saturday morning, and the weather was still nice, if a little cold, but I didn't see anyone else nearby. That was good. I needed to talk to someone about everything that was going on in my head, and I didn't want anyone overhearing. I could've talked to Jenna, and I probably would at some point, but not today.

The grass was damp, but I sat down anyway. I doubted I'd feel it through my jeans, but even if I did, a little discomfort wasn't my primary concern.

"There aren't a whole lot of sunflowers around Halloween," I continued. "I'll bring some in this spring, or whenever they bloom."

I crossed my legs and leaned forward, resting my elbows on my knees. The irony of the moment wasn't lost on me. When Adare had been alive, I hadn't told her about my past. She could've looked into it, but I knew she hadn't. She would've wanted me to come to her myself.

"I'm sorry," I said as I pulled up a couple blades of grass and rolled them between my fingers. "I should've told you everything. You wouldn't have pitied me or looked at me differently. I was just scared." I sighed. "No, that's not the truth. Not the whole truth anyway. I was scared, but it had nothing to do with me worrying about how you would have seen or treated me. It was all me. I'm terrified of my past. I don't want to have to think or talk about it. I just want to pretend that nothing happened."

I ran my hand over the grass and let my thoughts wander for a few minutes.

"Jalen and I are dating. I think." I smiled. "I know what you'd tell me about that. Either we are or we aren't, and if I don't know, I need to do something about it. But I'm scared of that too. What if I ask him and he says that we're not dating? What if I'm doing the same thing with him that I was doing with Clay, except this time, it's not my decision?"

I rubbed my forehead, but it didn't do much to help the throbbing.

"I want more than just a fuck buddy. But I also don't want more. What I had with Clay was good. Couldn't I have the same thing with Jalen? No risk of getting too close. We both walk away when we're done."

I didn't need Adare to be here to know what her response would've been.

"I know, I know," I said, pulling up another blade of grass. "I'll never move forward if I'm not willing to risk being hurt." I sighed. "Whenever people hear about my past, or even learn that I don't have any family, or discover that I wanted to join the FBI, or how I moved here on my own without knowing anyone, they'd tell me how brave I was. But I'm not brave. I'm scared of so much."

I didn't say anything else for a long while, and I tried not to think anything either. I let my mind go as blank as I could, skipping across thoughts without allowing myself to go any deeper. It helped that it was peaceful here.

When I finally got to my feet, I hadn't come up with any solutions or decisions, but I felt better anyway. If I got to a place where I needed actual advice, I'd probably go to Jenna. Considering she'd chewed Jalen out the last time he behaved like an ass, I felt comfortable that she wouldn't pull any punches, and I needed someone who wouldn't use my past as an excuse to treat me like I was fragile. Sometimes, a scared person needed a kick in the ass more than a sympathetic ear.

I was halfway back to my car when my phone started to ring. As the theme to a certain popular science-fiction movie series blared from my purse, I fumbled with my zipper. I hadn't realized how cold I'd gotten until my fingers didn't want to cooperate. I finally managed to get my phone out, answering it without looking at the caller ID.

"Hello?"

"You have a collect call from Indiana State Prison."

I went numb, barely hearing my father saying his name during the pause in the robotic statement. I ended the call and dropped my phone back into my purse. For nearly ten years, he'd sat in prison and left me alone. I'd ignored him at the trial *and* made a point of testifying against him.

What in the *hell* had given him the idea that I'd accept a collect call from him, let alone actually want to talk to him?

SEVEN

"It's the gall of him that I just can't get over," I said, shaking my head. "I mean, when he had his accident, I couldn't completely understand what happened, but I was old enough to get that a brain injury could change a person. It was still awful, and he deserves to be in prison for life, but..."

I ran both of my hands through my hair, unable to come up with the words to explain what I was really feeling.

Jalen found the words that I couldn't. "But while he was in prison, states away, not reaching out to you, not *present*, it was easier to accept that the father you'd known wasn't the father who'd done those horrible things." His voice softened. "But it wasn't him then, and it still isn't him now. The man who raised you, who loved you, it's not the same man."

My eyes burned. "I know."

He stood up and came around the table. As he knelt

next to me, he took my hands in his. "You don't owe *this* man anything. Don't let what you felt for the man from your childhood make you feel like you need to love the man in prison."

The truth of what he said took a weight off of me that I hadn't realized I was carrying. I needed to look at the man who'd killed my mother, killed those other people, tried to kill me, as someone completely separate from my father. I needed to allow myself to be free to feel the same thing for present-day Willis Jacobe that I would have felt if he had been a neighbor, an acquaintance, a complete stranger.

It'd take some time, but at least I had a goal now.

"Thank you," I said. I put my hands on his cheeks and leaned forward, pressing my lips against his. "I needed that."

He smiled at me, those gorgeous eyes of his glowing. "Anytime." He stood and held out a hand. "What do you say we go find a movie to watch and leave the clean-up until tomorrow?"

I took his hand and let him help me to my feet. I wasn't about to go telling everyone about my past, but I had to admit that it was nice being able to talk to someone who knew it all.

And he didn't look bad when he was listening either.

Hell, he didn't look bad when he was doing anything, really.

We settled on the couch, and I leaned against him, content to let him decide what to watch. I wasn't really in the mood to concentrate on anything, but I knew Jalen wouldn't be offended if I dozed or simply let my mind drift.

I'd done a little of both for at least an hour when I found something else to focus on. Namely, the way Jalen's thumb had been moving back and forth across my upper arm for the past quarter hour. Warmth spread across my skin, pooled low in my belly.

I'd been resting with my head on his chest, and now I slid my hand across his stomach. As I moved under his shirt, palm skimming over hard muscles, his thumb stopped moving.

"Babe?"

I pushed up his shirt and pressed my lips against his bare skin. He shifted, grabbing my shoulders and pulling me up so that we were face-to-face. He cupped my chin, and while his grip was a little too tight to be comfortable, but the moment I saw how his eyes were blazing, I didn't care.

"If I kiss you now, will I be taking advantage of you?"

Fuck, I hoped so.

I leaned forward, but he held me in place.

"You and I are going to have a serious discussion about you thinking you're in control here." His voice was low, sensual. "Because we both know who's in charge."

"Yes, Sir." I grabbed the front of his shirt. "Now, tell me what to do."

He pulled me onto his lap, his mouth claiming mine even as his hands settled on my hips. I'd worn pants this evening, but I was starting to regret that particular wardrobe choice. The jeans were comfortable, but as I straddled Jalen's lap, they put too many layers between us. I kept telling myself that we needed to work on building something between us that wasn't sex, but my libido hadn't gotten the message yet.

His hands slid up my sides and under my shirt. I squirmed as his palms skimmed my ribcage, and he chuckled. One hand moved to my back, holding me in place as he pulled my bottom lip into his mouth, teeth worrying at it even as I ground down on his lap, wanting to feel as much of him as I could.

I pushed my hands under his shirt again, his skin hot under my palms. Would I ever get tired of the way he felt? The way he looked? I didn't think so. His touch made me weak in the knees, and whenever I was with him, I wanted to touch him.

It would've been embarrassing if I hadn't seen other people look at him the same way I did. He was the sort of man who could take a person's breath away, but he wasn't only an Adonis. He had an intelligence that made him one of the top minds in the country, if not the world, and a depth that few would've credited him with.

But other people didn't get to touch him. I did.

He palmed the back of my head as he broke the kiss, his fingers rubbing against my scalp as if he felt the same need I did, to get closer, to imprint the feel of my body on his fingertips. His forehead came to rest on mine, his breathing as ragged as mine.

"Fuck, Rona, what do you do to me?" His voice was a low rumble through me. "I can't get you out of my head. When I'm not with you, I'm thinking about you.

Thinking about touching you, about what it's like to be inside you."

I made a soft sound, flexing my fingers against his stomach until my nails bit into his skin, and he growled. "I'm always thinking about you too," I confessed. "It's never...I've never..."

I didn't know the words to explain what I was feeling because I'd never felt anything like it before. Not with anyone, not even Clay. It should have terrified me, and it probably would when I thought about it later, but right now, I had this nearly overwhelming need for him to know that whatever this was between us was different.

A door slammed, jerking us both out of the intimate bubble we'd had around us.

"Jalen!"

I started to move off his lap, my gut telling me that I didn't want whoever that was to find the two of us like this. Jalen wrapped his arm around my waist, holding me on his lap. His expression was blank, almost relaxed. If I hadn't felt the tension radiating off him, I wouldn't have suspected anything was wrong.

"Jalen!"

She stepped into the living room a split second before I realized her identity.

A couple inches shorter than my own five feet, ten inches, Elise Marx was on the shorter end for a model, but that hadn't kept her from having a great career for the last ten years. I didn't have anything against models. Most of them were as responsible for their thin bodies and fine features as I was for my own athletic build. Still, there was something about the way she carried herself that just rubbed me the wrong way.

"Who the fuck are you?" She glared down at me. Her dark eyes narrowed. "Wait a minute. I've seen you before. You said you were here to talk to him about some other bitch he was fucking."

I was aware that my mouth was hanging open, but I couldn't seem to do anything to stop it. This woman was caustic.

"Elise, you're not supposed to be here." His hand tightened on my hip. "This isn't your home anymore."

"Of course not," she said, stalking over to us. "How can it be my home if you've already replaced me with this slut?"

He had me off his lap and onto the couch before I'd even realized he was moving me. He stood, towering over her even as he stepped between the two of us. "That's enough, Elise."

"I haven't said nearly enough." She put her hands on her hips and glowered up at him. "I put up with you wanting to live here when it hurt my career. I held my tongue when you wanted a separation, and again when you filed for divorce. But this, *this* is too far. I won't be made a fool of."

She made as if to move around him, but he sidestepped, getting between us again. Her expression twisted into something ugly, and one hand flashed out. Before it could land on his cheek, he caught her around the wrist. Nothing about his appearance changed, but I could feel a shift in the air.

"I think you should go." Jalen didn't raise his voice, but then again, he rarely needed to.

I couldn't stop a smug smile. Maybe it was rude of me, but I was beginning to think she was one of those people who didn't respond to subtlety.

She began, "Jalen–"

"Rona, you should go."

Time froze for a moment as a rush of humiliation washed over me. He wanted me to go. She showed up uninvited, interrupting a date, and he wanted *me* to go.

I didn't look at Elise as I got up, but I could feel her watching me. I didn't look at Jalen either, but a part of me didn't truly believe that he was going to let me walk out without a word until I was actually standing next to my car.

As I drove home, I kept telling myself that neither Jalen nor I had talked about whether or not we were exclusive. I had no right to be upset. We hadn't established what we were to each other. Neither of us had any claim on the other.

The problem was, it didn't do anything to make me hurt less.

EIGHT

I WAS GRATEFUL FOR THE WORK JENNA HAD GIVEN ME. Without it, I would've gone crazy.

I spent Sunday putting together all the information I'd gathered when looking for Meka, including my less-than-orthodox 'interview' with Meka's ex-boyfriend Shawn. I doubted I had much of anything that the FBI didn't already have, but I figured if I gave it to Jenna, she could determine whether or not to pass the information along.

It might also give her somewhere to look that she hadn't thought of yet. With Shawn's age, I had no doubt his social media accounts would provide a plethora of information. Whether or not any of it would be useful was anybody's guess.

I'd taken her the information first thing this morning, then headed up to Cheyenne. The US Marshals hadn't been too keen on talking to me over the phone, but that didn't mean an in-person visit would yield the same results. During the hour drive, I called Clay – hands-free of course – to ask for a name. That name was the reason I'd been sitting outside an apartment building since noon.

Clay hadn't been able to tell me much, and I hadn't pressed him to give me anything but the name and where I could find him. I didn't want to risk my friend's career, but part of being in any sort of investigative field often meant calling in favors. Considering the help I'd be giving Jenna – and through her, Clay and his partner – I didn't feel overly guilty for the request.

I'd done a little general internet searching while I waited, which had given me a wedding announcement from twenty-seven years ago and not much else. The fact that it was a Monday and I was sitting in front of an apartment instead of going into the local law enforcement office made me think that maybe Harry Franklin had retired.

Clay had sent over a picture, so when the silver-haired man in a cheap suit came out of the building, I recognized him. He looked a few years older than the picture, but still in his mid to late fifties, which meant it hadn't been too long since he'd been with the Marshal service.

I hurried after him, careful to keep back a few feet until he ducked into a diner. I didn't want a big public confrontation, but I didn't want to corner him somewhere we'd be completely alone either. I doubted Clay would give me the name of someone who'd be a danger to me, but people did strange things when they felt threatened, and I had no way of knowing if asking about Jenna's mother would come across as a threat.

He settled into a booth at the back of the diner and

ordered some coffee. I waited until the waitress left before I slid into the empty space across from him.

"Mr. Franklin?"

The look he gave me was shrewd, careful. He knew I wasn't here to sell him life insurance or whatever sort of things salespeople sold face-to-face. Straightforward would be the best approach, I decided on the spot. I just hoped my gut was right about that.

"My name's Rona Quick, and I'm a private investigator."

He stiffened but didn't leave or tell me to get lost. Instead, he sipped his coffee and waited.

"I was hired to look into a woman who went by the name Helen Kingston, though you'd know her as Anna Newbury or Marcy Wakefield."

His lips pressed together in a thin line, all pretense of casual vanishing. "Miss Quick, I'm going to advise you to walk out of here and forget those names. You tell whoever hired you that looking for that woman is pointless."

I folded my hands in front of me, giving him my best polite smile. I paused to let the returning waitress take our orders and then vanish into the kitchen. "Here's the thing, Mr. Franklin. I know that Marcy was the alias Anna was given when she entered WITSEC thirteen years ago. Before that, she'd used the names Helen Kingston and Helena King. When she was arrested years ago on multiple charges of child pornography – among other things – she gave up names in order to stay out of prison."

"You shouldn't know any of that," he said.

I shrugged. "Probably not, but it became pretty

common knowledge down in Fort Collins when Marcy came after one of her many children. Specifically, the daughter who was responsible for her first arrest. After that, she didn't get any plea deals. She's in prison for a long time."

He took another drink of his coffee. "Then you should know that you need to contact the Department of Corrections to find her."

"You misunderstand," I said. "I'm not looking for her, but rather for the children she had while she was in WITSEC."

The coffee cup clattered as he set it back on the saucer, a little liquid slopping over the top.

"That woman ruined my career when she took off," he said. "Why should I get involved in anything to do with her?"

A few pieces fell into place, enough for me to feel comfortable making a logical leap. "Because you're the Marshal who made a formal request for the higher-ups to do something about the fact that a known child abuser kept having kids."

"Where did you hear that?" he asked, just sharply enough for me to know that my hunch was right on target.

"You had to have read her file." I kept going without answering his question. "You knew what she'd done to the one daughter she hadn't given away. When did you first find out that she was pregnant?"

He didn't say anything at first, but I allowed the silence to keep growing. It was his move now. If I had to push more, I would, but it would be best if this was his choice.

Finally, he relented. "Three weeks after she arrived here, I found a pregnancy test in her bathroom. It wasn't until later that I realized she'd left it there on purpose. I was hard on her when we first met, and I think she'd thought that knowing she was pregnant would soften me up."

"But it didn't."

He shook his head. "But she used it to manipulate me for more lax monitoring. All she'd had to do was make a casual comment about knowing people who'd love a baby, and I was picturing all of the crime scene photos from her file."

I muttered a curse. It shouldn't have surprised me, not when I knew what she'd done to Jenna, but I could apparently still be shocked by how much of a monster Helen was.

He lifted his mug but didn't take a sip. "I talked her into putting the baby up for adoption."

"I spoke with a social worker who confirmed as much," I said. "But I'd never be able to get details without a warrant."

"Why do you want details?" His guard came up again. "Are the children's fathers coming forward?"

I debated for a moment, then answered, "No, their sister. Half-sister. The one Helen kept."

"She wants to find the kids?" He sounded genuinely surprised.

"My client would like to have the opportunity to get to know as many of her siblings as she can. She'd like a relationship with them if at all possible but will settle for the knowledge that they're safe."

The waitress returned with our food, and we both fell silent as we ate. The fact that Harry blamed Marcy for his 'retirement' could've made him bitter and unwilling to help. Instead, I was getting the impression that he wanted to do whatever possible to make sure that Marcy's kids didn't suffer any more ill effects from their mother's choices. His reluctance to talk was because he wanted to protect them, not himself.

"I checked up on the kids she had while in the program," he finally admitted. "The first couple years anyway. I wanted to make sure they were being treated well."

My heart picked up speed. "Does that mean you know where they are?"

He shook his head. "Sorry, kid. I know a few things here and there, but I don't have an address for any of them. I paid a social worker to give me what she could without getting herself into too much trouble. Not much, but enough to know that the kids were okay."

I pulled out my notebook and pen, my meal forgotten. "All right. What can you tell me?"

AS I DROVE BACK to Fort Collins, I vacillated between frustration and satisfaction. My trip hadn't been useless. I'd gotten information that I couldn't have found anywhere else, and I was confident that I'd be able to use it to find

Jenna's brothers and sister. It wasn't the lack of even more details that had me frowning.

Harry had taken the brunt of the responsibility for Helen's escape, but in my opinion, it had been the justice system as a whole that had failed Jenna. Helen might have given the names of some men who'd raped Jenna and those who'd been involved in the recordings she'd helped make, but I couldn't understand how anyone had been okay with making a deal with her, let alone letting her be the one to decide whether or not to keep the children who'd been born while she was in WITSEC.

Three children for certain, but one of the new things I'd learned today made me think that there might be a fourth out there.

Helen's appearance in Fort Collins wasn't the first time she'd slipped Marshal custody. Eight years ago, Harry had caught Helen hiding a third pregnancy. She'd been furious enough that he'd suspected she was up to no good. His suspicions had been confirmed when she'd taken off a few weeks later. He'd been embarrassed enough by her getting past him that he'd looked for her himself rather than telling his superiors that he'd lost her. Two weeks later, she'd returned, no longer pregnant. She told him that she'd taken a trip with a couple friends and had forgotten to tell him. While on the trip, she'd gone into labor. The baby had been stillborn.

Worried about his job, he'd let the matter go, but he hadn't ever really been able to forget. Even now, he suspected that the baby hadn't died, but hadn't done anything about it. He'd been too much of a fucking coward then, and he was still one now. My original thought that he'd been protecting the kids had only been partially right. Covering his own ass had been more important than doing the right thing. If Clay hadn't given me Harry's name, I doubted he would've told anyone the whole story.

Yet another reason I hadn't been able to thoroughly enjoy the fact that I'd gotten a good lead on the other kids.

I just needed to remember to take things one step at a time. I'd do everything in my power to find every one of the kids, but it was going to be a long process. I couldn't let myself get discouraged, or I'd never get through it.

I'D FOUND HER. At least, I was fairly certain that I had.

I leaned back in my chair and stared at my computer screen, reviewing the facts that Harry and twelve hours of research had brought me. I'd worked until the early hours of the morning, managed a couple hours of restless sleep, and then got up just after sunrise to continue working.

The girl had turned thirteen on August seventeenth. The name Marcy Wakefield was on the birth certificate, and the father had been listed as unknown. While the father's race hadn't been recorded either, Harry had been present when the girl had been handed over to Child and Family Services, and he'd been able to tell me that whoever the man was, he'd given his daughter milk chocolate skin and raven-black curls.

Harry had also told me that the girl had been named Stacey, and shortly before the adoption proceedings were concluded, her family told the social worker that they would be moving to Loveland, Colorado after everything was finalized. That had been the last he'd heard other than a general report the following year that she was doing well.

That information had been enough for me to find Stacey Johnson, daughter of Elliot and Roberta Johnson, a resident of a city less than thirty miles south of where her sister had been living for years. She was an eighth-grader in the local high school and had started an anti-bullying campaign that was now in its second year.

Those particular details had been revealed by something so technologically simple that I hadn't needed to contact Jenna to do her hacking thing. I'd done a social media search. It'd taken a while to weed through all the possibilities, but it'd been worth it. Once I'd gotten everyone's names, it'd been relatively simple to find an address.

Scarily simple, actually.

I was suddenly grateful that I'd never gotten into the whole social media thing. It would've been far too easy for reporters to track me down here.

I printed out the page and then looked at the time. Mid-afternoon. I was already exhausted, but I wouldn't be able to rest if I knew I had this information here and Jenna had waited for years for it.

I texted her first to see if it'd be okay if I came by, and as soon as she said yes, I was in my car. I told myself I was doing this because I wanted her to know as soon as possible. It had nothing to do with the fact that it'd been three days since Jalen had told me to leave his house and he hadn't made an attempt to contact me at all.

I supposed I could have reached out to him first, but considering that he'd chosen his *wife* over me, I felt I was justified in wanting him to come to me.

But that wasn't why I was going to Jenna now.

And at some point today, I might actually believe it.

Jenna looked surprisingly calm when she opened the door, but once we were seated in the kitchen, I noticed that she kept fiddling with her sleeve. Specifically, the part covering her scar. The scar she'd gotten when she tried to kill herself as a child.

Was she wondering if I was going to give her bad news? Tell her that the people who'd adopted one of her sisters had done the same sort of awful things that she'd had done to her?

I'd had some really shitty stuff happen to me in my life, but even knowing the little bit that I did about what'd happened to her made my own background almost happy by comparison. At least I had twelve years of great family memories.

"I have some information for you," I said. "Do you want me to tell you or do you want to read yourself?"

"Tell me." She stared at her hands. "I'm not sure I could absorb it if I had to read it."

I gave her everything I had, keeping things simple. I didn't slow things down, but I didn't try to rush through it either. She needed me to be solid if things hit her hard.

For the first time, I wondered if I should have waited for Rylan to be here to help her through it, but I knew I had to trust that she would've said something if she needed his presence.

When I finished, I leaned back in my chair and waited for her to process. I'd never done this before, been there for a friend. Not because I wouldn't have wanted to be there for someone, but because I'd never had a friend like this. Clay had been the closest thing, but we'd never really talked about anything personal. Asking about his past had always felt dishonest to me, considering I didn't want him to ask about mine.

I could do it now, I realized. I could ask him whatever I wanted because he already knew all the worst parts of my life.

"Stacey," Jenna said finally. "I have a sister named Stacey."

"I'm going to keep looking for the others," I said. "When you're ready, we'll talk about the direction you want to take with each of them."

"Does she know she's adopted?"

"I don't know. She actually resembles her mother – the woman who adopted her, I mean. She doesn't look anything like Helen."

"That's a relief," Jenna said. "I'm bracing myself to see a picture of one of them and see our mother looking back at me."

I went on my phone and pulled up the picture I'd downloaded. "Here."

Jenna stared down at the screen. "Those are her parents?" She smiled softly. "You're right. She looks like her mom, only a bit darker. Same nose and chin."

"Everything I've found on them so far has been great.

A real solid family. I'll take a closer look at them in real life, but it's promising."

"I'd like to meet her," Jenna said suddenly. "Do you think her parents would let me?"

The hope in her eyes twisted my heart. I knew what it was like to want something so badly that it hurt.

"I don't know. Do you want me to talk to them on your behalf?"

"I think that'd be best," she said. "Don't you? They don't know that the name on Stacey's birth certificate is fake. If I go, there will be questions, and I don't think that's the best way for me to introduce myself."

"All right," I agreed. "I'll call them in a bit and set up a time to meet. I'll let you know as soon as I get things scheduled."

"Thank you." She got up and got us both a bottle of beer. When she sat back down, she gave me a searching look. "Now, what's wrong?"

I almost spit out my beer. "Excuse me?"

"You were very professional," she said with a half-smile, "but I've gotten to know you over the last couple weeks, and I can see past that smile. What's wrong?"

I swallowed hard at the lump that suddenly formed in my throat. I'd spent so much of my life having to do things alone. With Jenna, I'd never need to worry that she'd be freaked out by anything she learned about me, and she'd never push when I wasn't ready to talk.

Unless pushing was exactly what I needed.

"Talk to me."

"Jalen." I took a long drink. "The short version is that

we were together, his wife came over, and he told me to leave. He picked her over me and hasn't called me for three days."

Jenna shook her head. "Men can be such idiots."

"Amen to that," I muttered.

"Piece of advice from someone who fought against love." She leaned forward. "Take it easy on him. It's as hard for him as it is for you."

NINE

I HADN'T GIVEN THE JOHNSONS MUCH OVER THE phone, and maybe that made me a bad person, but I knew it'd be easier for them to turn me away if we were on the phone than when we were face-to-face. I'd abide by whatever their answer was, but I intended to make sure they at least heard everything I had to say first.

I was just glad they'd agreed to see me so soon. I was grateful for the distraction, and I didn't want to make Jenna wait any longer than she had to.

Their house was nice, I thought as I walked up to it. A good, solid middle-class family home. Stacey was fortunate to have grown up there.

It wasn't until I was raising my hand to knock that I realized the impact my news was going to have on this family. I'd been so focused on what it meant for Jenna that I hadn't stopped to think about Stacey or her parents. Telling them that Stacey's half-sister wanted to meet her would change their lives, no matter what they decided.

Before I could knock – and before I could change my mind – the door opened, and a handsome Haitian man greeted me.

"Ms. Quick?"

"Yes." I held out my hand, and he shook it. "Mr. Johnson, I presume."

"Come on in." He stepped back to give me room, and then I followed him into the living room where a pretty, dark-haired woman was waiting. "My wife, Roberta."

"Nice to meet you." I shook her hand as well.

Once we'd all taken our seats, Elliot reached over and took Roberta's hand. The two of them looked like they were bracing themselves, and I hoped that what I had to tell them wouldn't be as bad as what they'd clearly been imagining.

"You said you wanted to talk to us about our daughter," he said. I could hear a faint French accent to his words. Or something close to French at least.

"I need to confirm a couple things first," I said. I was almost one hundred percent sure that Stacey was Jenna's sister, but I'd be a horrible PI if I didn't verify. "Stacey turned thirteen on August seventeenth, correct?"

They both nodded.

"And you adopted her as a baby?"

They both stiffened, and I felt the mood in the room shift. They'd been worried before. Now, they were guarded too.

"I don't see how that's any of your business," Roberta said tightly.

It was time to lay my cards on the table. "I'm a private

investigator, hired by a woman who may be Stacey's half-sister."

They looked at each other before Roberta spoke. "The adoption was closed, and from the little we were told, it was arranged that way to protect Stacey from her biological family."

"From her mother, yes. If Stacey is the young woman I've been looking for, then keeping her from any contact with her biological mother is a good thing. Her half-siblings, however, may or may not present any issues. I was hired to find all of Marcy Wakefield's children."

Roberta flinched as soon as I said the name, the last confirmation that I needed. "We don't know anything about that woman or her family. We won't put our daughter into that situation."

"I understand," I said as sympathetically as I could. I needed to be diplomatic here, take their very valid concerns seriously. "And I can't vouch for any of the other siblings, but the woman who hired me, she's a good person. She's twenty-six, married with two adopted children. They have a comfortable life. She has no desire to complicate things with your daughter. She just wants to know her brothers and sisters."

Elliot shook his head. "There must be some mistake."

"I'm sorry, Mr. Johnson, but if Marcy Wakefield is Stacey's biological mother, then she is my client's sister." I looked up at the family portrait hanging on the wall across from me. "She just wants to know her family."

"*We* are Stacey's only family," Roberta said sharply.

"It's been thirteen years, and we haven't heard a peep until now."

I chose my next words carefully. Jenna hadn't given me any restrictions as to what I could tell the Johnsons, but I knew if our situations were reversed, I'd want Jenna to be as tactful as possible. Then there was the fact that if I revealed too much, I'd bring Archer Enterprises into the picture, and I didn't know enough about the two people sitting across from me to determine if they'd make any sort of meeting contingent upon payment. My gut told me they were decent people looking out for their daughter, but my views on parenting were colored by my past.

"Marcy Wakefield wasn't her real name. She was in witness protection, and that was the new name she was given after she provided the Florida DA with the names of people who trafficked in some pretty nasty stuff."

I'd let their imagination do the work for them. I didn't know everything Jenna's mother had done, but I didn't doubt that it was far more depraved than what most people ever wanted to consider. Roberta's face paled until I could see freckles that I hadn't noticed before.

"My client is one of eleven children Marcy gave birth to, but the only one she kept for more than a few months. To guard my client's privacy, I won't tell you about the quality of her life in the thirteen years she was with her biological mother, but I will say that it is more horrific than you would want to envision."

"*Cher Dieu.*" Elliot's words sounded like a prayer.

I nodded. Dear god indeed. "It's taken my client years

to deal with her childhood, and now that she's healthy enough to be a parent, she wants to be a sister too."

"We never met Marcy Wakefield," Roberta said, "but I'd always assumed she'd been an addict. Maybe a prostitute. But what you said..." She shook her head, looking as is she was searching for the right word.

"She's in prison now." I leaned forward, bracing my elbows on my knees. "I can't go into details, but suffice it to say that she violated her agreement with the justice department and has been put away for a long time. You'll never need to worry about her contacting Stacey."

"We just need to worry about your client then, is that right?" Elliot's tone wasn't rude, but it definitely wasn't friendly either. "Our daughter doesn't know that she's adopted, but even if she did, I wouldn't want her to meet any of her biological family, no matter how together they are now."

I should've kept my mouth shut, but the question popped out anyway. "Are you ever going to tell her?"

"Not that it's any of your business, young lady," Roberta said, lifting her chin, "but no. I have a cousin who was adopted and had been told so from moment one. When he was a teenager, it came between him and his parents, to the point where he would threaten to find his 'real' parents every time he didn't like what they told him to do or not do. He's twenty-seven now and has nothing to do with any of us."

Shit. With something like that affecting her judgment, she wasn't going to relent any time soon, and certainly not if I kept pushing.

"Thank you for meeting me," I said as I stood. "I appreciate you talking to me, and I'll advise my client regarding your decision." I took a business card from my pocket and handed it to Elliot. "Should you change your mind, please call me."

"We won't," Roberta said firmly. "I'm sorry you came here for nothing."

So was I, especially since I had to go tell my friend that the one sibling I'd found was one she'd probably never get to meet.

This was going to suck.

TEN

I REALLY DIDN'T WANT TO DO THIS.

If I didn't figure out a way to get past how much I hated delivering bad news, I had a feeling Burkart Investigations wouldn't last long. As much as I wished I could guarantee that I'd be able to solve every case I took on and do it in a way where no one would ever get hurt, it wasn't possible. Hell, most of my jobs would consist of me telling someone that their significant other was being unfaithful. Not exactly the stuff dreams were made of.

I texted Jenna to let her know I was coming by, and she'd said that was fine. She didn't ask what'd happened, and as I drove to her house, I wondered if she was trying to talk herself down from being too hopeful.

How shitty were our lives that we felt like we couldn't *hope* for something as simple as a relationship with a sister?

Jenna and Rylan's house impressed me every time I came. Maybe in a couple years, the massive mansion would just be my friends' house, and I wouldn't blink at the fact that my entire building could fit inside the house. Twice.

"Rona, nice to see you," Rylan said as he opened the door. His shirt was dusted with what looked like flour, and his sleeves were rolled up to his elbows. "Come on in. The kids and I are making pizza for dinner. Can I interest you in joining us?"

The offer threw me. "Uh, I'm just here to talk to Jenna, but if this is a bad time…?"

"Not at all," Rylan said with a smile. "It's my turn to take care of dinner tonight, which means she's either in the library with a new book or she's taking a bath."

"I'll check the library first." Since she knew I was coming, the library seemed like the best bet.

"Down the hall, second door on the right." Rylan gestured toward the hallway. "If she's not there, feel free to come back and help us with the pizzas until she's out of the tub."

I nodded and headed to the library, a massive room filled with more books than I could imagine reading in a lifetime. Jenna was curled up in a comfortable-looking armchair, a book on her lap. I doubted she was reading it though. Her expression was vacant, troubled, but as soon as she heard me, her head jerked up, her eyes wide.

"Hey." Her voice sounded strained. "You made good time."

"Traffic was light," I said as I took a seat in the chair across from her.

"It's not good news, is it?" she asked softly. "Did something happen to her?"

"No, no," I rushed to reassure her. "She's fine. Nice house. Good parents."

The relief on her face was obvious. "I know you'd said that before but..."

"Looks can be deceiving," I said. "I should know."

"But you still have bad news." She looked like she was bracing herself, and it killed me to know that what I had to tell her would hurt her.

"It's not great news," I admitted. "I confirmed that Stacey is your sister, but she doesn't know that she's adopted."

Jenna nodded as she folded her arms across her chest, one of those almost-unconscious movements that people made when they felt the need to protect themselves from some emotional threat.

"They don't want me to meet her."

"I'm so sorry, Jenna."

"I get it," she said. "They're her parents. They have the right to decide whether or not they tell her about the adoption. I show up, and she'll start asking questions that they're not going to want to answer."

She pushed herself out of the chair and walked over to the window. She didn't say anything as she stared outside, but I doubted she was seeing anything.

"I didn't tell them who you were," I said, "but I did give them an idea of who Marcy – Helen – was, and I told them a bit about you. About how you were a good person, had a family. I told them to contact me if they change their minds."

"You did the right thing," she said. "Telling them about

Helen. I doubt she'll ever try to contact any of them, but if by some strange fluke she does, at least her parents will know to keep Stacey away from her."

"They'll have to tell her the truth sometime," I said, "and maybe they'll change their mind. Rather than risking her trying to find Helen, they'll know they can reach out to you."

She didn't look at me. "Maybe."

After nearly a full minute of silence, I excused myself. As I came down the hall, I heard Rylan and the kids laughing. Such a light, happy sound. It seemed so out of place after the gloom in the library. I almost considered going back and telling Jenna to go be with her family, but I'd been in a similar place before. Sometimes, forcing in the light didn't push away the darkness. It just made it clear that sometimes there were places that even the light couldn't go.

I slipped out of the house without anyone seeing, not trusting myself to be able to be convincingly upbeat. When Jenna wanted to tell Rylan about what had happened, she'd do it. Until then, the best thing I could do was let Rylan take care of their kids so she could work out things in her own head.

I drove about a mile down the road before I realized that I didn't want to go home. I loved my apartment, but it was empty right now. As much as I usually liked having my own space, I needed to get out of my head, and I couldn't do that alone.

I didn't know many people in the city well enough to show up on their doorsteps, and with me coming from one of those places, it left me with only two options. Clay or Jalen.

It wasn't the nearly hour long drive to Clay that had me choosing to go to Jalen. We hadn't talked since the incident with Elise, but he was still the one I wanted. I *needed*. When I pulled up in front of his house, I wondered if I should have called first, but then the front door opened, and Jalen was there with a look of such relief that I knew I'd made the right decision.

Neither of us said anything as we made our way to the living room. I sat down next to him, close enough for our legs to touch, and wondered where to begin.

"I'm sorry," he said. "I should've called you."

"Yes." I was pleased with how steady my voice was. "You should have." I put my hand on his knee. "But I could've called you, and I didn't. Let's agree that we both should have reached out and let that go."

"I'd like that." He put his hand on mine. "I want to clear the air about everything."

"I'd like that." I tried not to let myself hope that things were going to be fixed between us with a single conversation. What I'd seen tonight was proof of how dangerous hope could be.

"I was trying to protect you."

"Protect me?" I wasn't following.

"I needed to get you away from Elise and telling her to leave would've just made things worse. She would only start coming after you, and I couldn't let that happen. Telling you to leave was the only way I could guarantee you wouldn't be a target."

Remembering how vicious she'd been, I could understand what he was saying. I didn't like it, and I had a couple questions, but all of the hurt and anger that I still had under the surface faded.

"Why didn't you call me that night and tell me all this? I would've understood."

He flipped my hand and threaded his fingers between mine. "Couple reasons, some of which sounded more reasonable than others at the time. The biggest one is that I was scared."

I squeezed his hand. It felt good to be touching him again. *Right.* "Scared of what?"

"Scared that you wouldn't believe me." His gaze caught mine. "Scared that Elise would keep coming after you. That she'd hurt you. Not physically. I don't think she'd do anything like that, but when it comes to the things that she says..."

His voice trailed off, but I could see the emotions playing across his face. He meant it. All of it. He should've called me, but his reasons made sense.

"I can handle anything she throws my way," I said quietly. "I appreciate what you were trying to do, but I refuse to let her behavior regulate my choices. If you want things between us to work out, you need to know that I don't expect you to protect me. I don't need it. If I ever do, I'll ask."

A little voice in the back of my mind asked if I was being honest. I wasn't exactly great at asking for help, even when I needed it. I meant it though. I wanted to be that person, the one who could actually have an equal partnership with someone.

He put his hand on my cheek, his thumb brushing against my skin. "I'll try to do better. I want this to work, Rona."

I leaned into his touch. "Me too."

He leaned forward, his lips grazing mine. It was barely a touch, but I felt it all the way down to my toes. Damn, I'd missed him. Missed this connection.

"Is this the only reason you came tonight or was there something else?"

I ran my hand over his cheek, enjoying the rough scruff against my palm. "I had to give a client some disappointing news, and when I left, I knew I didn't want to be alone. You were the only person I wanted to be with, and I was tired of waiting for you to make the first move."

He slid his hand around the back of my neck, his fingers strong and comforting. "I missed you so much."

His thumb rubbed the base of my skull, sending a shiver down my spine. This thing between us...it didn't seem to matter what we did or said, it kept pulling us together. Like magnets. Unable to resist the attraction. Not that I wanted to resist it. I was done trying to stay away, trying to explain it. From here on out, I was just going to accept it. Whatever work we needed to do, I'd do it.

"Tell me what you need," he said.

"Hold me."

His arms immediately wrapped around me, and he kissed the top of my head. "I've got you."

For the first time that week, I felt safe.

ELEVEN

It'd been late by the time I'd gotten home last night, but I'd needed to sleep in my own bed. I didn't want things between Jalen and me to always result in us falling into bed together. We'd made out a little bit, sure, but we hadn't had sex. I'd dreamed about it last night and woken up with my entire body throbbing with need.

Needless to say, my shower had been on the cold side, but at least I wasn't running late for lunch with Clay, *and* I'd gotten in a nice run before taking a second cold shower. My libido was in hiding at the moment, and I intended to keep it that way until I was done with work for the day. After that, all bets were off.

Clay had come down to Fort Collins to pick up some information from Jenna that he and Agent Matthews wanted in hard copy, which was perfect since that meant I could fill him in on my own contributions to the case. I hoped that common ground would keep things from being awkward between us since this was our first alone time since I'd gotten back from Indiana.

Snooze was one of my favorite places to eat in the city. I'd found it my second day here, and it'd become one of my go-to places to eat. I could cook well enough, but the time it took usually meant I didn't get into anything too complicated.

I arrived before Clay and took a booth close to the door, so he'd see me when he came in. My phone buzzed, and I picked it up. I smiled when I saw who it was from.

I'm supposed to be getting together specs for a lunch meeting, but you keep distracting me.

I tapped out a quick response. *How am I distracting you from all the way over here?*

It took him a minute to respond, and I found myself restlessly tapping the glass of water a waitress had brought over.

I keep thinking about what it would be like to take you in my office. Bent over my desk. Naked and spread open on top of my desk. Up against the door. In my chair. I'm hard as a fucking rock.

I flushed at the images his words prompted. We'd had sex on my desk – technically, it'd been Adare's desk at the time – and I still had moments where I'd zone out at work, the memories of that first time pushing every other thought out of my mind.

Don't expect any sympathy from me, I typed. *You've got me all hot and bothered now.*

"You look...busy."

I raised my head at the sound of Clay's voice. By the

time he was in the seat across from me, the waitress was there, taking his order for coffee and checking him out at the same time.

I watched, curious as to whether or not I'd feel even the tiniest prickle of jealousy. I hadn't had any issues with jealousy before, but when we'd started sleeping together, I had experienced a thrill of satisfaction when I'd seen women flirting with him. He'd been mine, and while we hadn't been dating, we had been exclusive. Now, however, there was nothing stopping him from meeting the waitress in the bathroom or behind the restaurant or whenever and wherever.

Nothing. I felt nothing more than a hope that he'd find the sort of happiness that Jalen and I had.

I quickly typed out another message. *Gotta go. Clay's here to go over case stuff. Rain check on finishing this conversation.*

I tucked my phone back into my purse and gave Clay my full attention. At least as much attention as I could give considering how turned on I was. A run and two cold showers for nothing. Damn Jalen for getting me all worked up.

"It's nothing important," I said. "Just talking to Jalen a bit while I was waiting."

I watched him carefully for any sign of annoyance or hurt, but he just smiled at me and took a long drink of his coffee. I could see the steam rising off of it, but he didn't even wince.

"How's business going?" he asked.

"Great," I said. Then I sighed. "Actually, I'm not sure if *great* is the right word."

"What happened?"

"I have one case at the moment, and it's a huge one, so money isn't the issue."

Or it wouldn't be when I got around to sending Jenna an invoice for hours worked. I could've done it earlier this week after I'd talked to Stacey's parents, but it'd felt wrong to charge her for shitty news.

Then again, knowing that Stacey existed and was with a solid, caring family was good news, and either way, Jenna wouldn't hold it against me.

"I had to deliver bad news," I said, giving him a wry smile. "I hadn't gotten to that part of my FBI training before I...left."

"Do you know what you want, or do you need more time?" The waitress gave Clay a winning smile and then turned it on me.

I ordered pancakes even though it was a little past noon and Clay asked for a bacon cheeseburger with a side of fries. When she walked back to the kitchen, I shifted the conversation. I didn't mind talking about the business, but I didn't want to give Clay enough to figure out my client was Jenna. I intended to take the privacy of all my clients seriously, but Jenna was also a friend.

"Jenna has me doing some research for her," I began, "on some people she's looking into for human trafficking."

Something flickered in his eyes, but his expression didn't change. "You're involved in one of her cases."

"She said she sends the information to Agent

Matthews. I'm guessing that means he shares it with you too."

He nodded slowly. "He does. We build cases with the information Jenna gets us." He shifted in his seat. "Are you sure it's a good idea to help her?"

I frowned. "Are you really asking me that? Is it a good idea to stop people who are kidnapping and selling human beings? What the hell kind of question is that?"

My voice rose on the last question, but I caught myself before it became too noticeable.

"Hey, hey," he held up his hands. "I'm just trying to look out for you."

"What is it with you men thinking I can't take care of myself?" I shook my head as I leaned back, crossing my arms. "Jalen did the same thing. Insults under the guise of protection."

"And what if you need our protection?" Clay countered.

"I'll ask."

He sighed. "Fair enough."

"Now, can we talk about work?" I gave him a hard look.

How he responded here would determine where things went from here, and my stomach twisted into knots at the thought of not having him in my life, but we needed to have this conversation.

"We can." He mimicked my posture. "Just promise me you'll be careful. That's all I ask." He gave me a half-smile. "I'd say the same thing to anyone else doing what you're doing."

"I am," I promised. "Jenna and I both are."

"Jenna handles things online," he pointed out. "You're actually going out and doing things. Besides, Rylan could kick the ass of anyone who tried to come after her."

He had a point.

"Jenna found the addresses." I moved the conversation along. "Usually, she can get camera footage online, but these were in blind spots. I gave her the photographs I already took, but I'm going back soon to take some more. I think they're rotating where they're keeping the people."

"Raymond thinks the same thing," Clay agreed. "We're trying to get IDs on the guys who are renting the locations."

As we settled into the conversation, the edge between us softened, and I knew we were going to be all right.

TWELVE

Thanksgiving was next week. It didn't seem possible that we were heading into the holiday season. Even the more frequent flurries couldn't make it feel real.

Holidays were hard. An understatement, really, but it wasn't like anyone could blame me. After my mom died, Uncle Anton and I had come up with our own traditions and ways to celebrate that let us remember without sadness taking over. Then he was gone, and I was alone.

As much as Clay looked after me, I'd always made sure he knew I had plans for the holidays. I never did, of course, but I wasn't about to let him make us both uncomfortable by asking me to spend the time with him and his family. Hell, I wouldn't have wanted an invitation even if he hadn't been the son of a congressman.

This year, I didn't know what I was going to do. Clay wouldn't be a problem. He'd assume that I was spending my days with Jalen, and I wasn't going to do anything to dissuade him. I was hoping that Jalen would assume I would be with Clay, but if he didn't, I needed to have a plan in place. I didn't want pity invites.

I was staring at the calendar, frowning as I counted the days between now and Thanksgiving, when I heard the front door shut. I straightened in the chair and put on my best professional look.

"Come on back," I called.

My first walk-in client.

If he hadn't been a man in his late fifties with thinning gray hair, a bit of a paunch, and a leer that he didn't even try to hide, I might've jumped up to shake his hand. Instead, I gestured to the chair across from me and told myself to ignore the suspicious-looking stain on his pants. The guy was probably just having a bad day. And he probably wasn't staring at my breasts. He was probably just...

Nope.

He was *definitely* staring at my breasts.

Still, I stayed polite. "Sir? Can I help you?"

"I hope so."

If he propositioned me, I was going to need a lawyer to get me out of what I did next. And possibly an alibi.

"My name's Evan Lee." He grinned at me with an expectant look on his face. When I just raised an eyebrow, his arrogant expression faltered. "I own Lee Automotive."

I knew of it, but only from the television ads. They were badly written, and the women on them looked as if he'd hired them straight off a porn set. Not really the most politically correct advertisements.

But none of that was a good excuse for kicking him out

before I heard what he had to say. "How can I help you, Mr. Lee?"

"I think my wife's cheating on me." He sighed as he dropped into the chair. "Hard to believe, right?"

Not so much. "You'd like me to follow her, find out one way or the other?"

He nodded. "I want to hire you to find out who she's fu–" his eyes dropped to my chest again as he cleared his throat, "who she's sleeping with so I can get her to divorce me without getting a single penny."

As much as I didn't like this guy, if he passed the background check I was going to do on him, I saw nothing to prevent me from taking the job. If I found out he had a single domestic assault charge, however, I would offer his wife the opportunity to get enough shit on him to be safe. Part of me didn't want to tell him about the background check, but I did it with all my other clients, which meant I had to do it here too.

"Before I take on any sort of domestic case, I do a background check on my client. This is your opportunity to tell me if I'm going to find anything that would make me think twice about tracking your wife."

He shrugged. "Got some parking tickets. Couple barroom fights that landed me in jail for a night."

He sounded sincere. Probably a creep, but not an abusive one.

"Do you have a picture of your wife?" I asked.

"Sure." He pulled out his phone, tapped the screen, then held it out.

I should've anticipated that the picture of his wife was

going to be naked, but I didn't. I managed not to react as I made a mental list of her appearance. Mid-forties, blonde hair that was obviously dyed. Brown or hazel eyes. Pretty, but worn.

"Thank you," I said as I handed him his phone back. "Now, if I can get some information from you, I can come up with a plan of action."

Two hours later, I was standing in front of the giant whiteboard, looking at the plan I'd come up with. He'd given me his address, as well as the address of where his wife worked, along with her schedule. Jessica worked as a receptionist for a doctor, which meant there was a possibility that she was cheating with someone at work. I'd need to research the doctor and the employees a bit, see how viable that particular avenue might be.

I'd start simple, the obvious places, following her when she left work or home. Once I figured out–

My phone rang, cutting into my concentration. I answered it without looking at the screen.

"Hello?"

"You have a collect call from Indiana State Prison."

I yanked the phone away from my ear and let out a string of curses. What the *hell* was he thinking?! I didn't want anything to do with him. I hadn't answered the last three calls. Why did he think I would answer this one?

I threw my pen across the room.

This needed to stop.

THIRTEEN

This was weird.

Like 'I couldn't believe I was doing this' weird.

I was in a new dress. Something nice, but not too fancy. Three-quarter sleeves. A neckline that almost showed a hint of my scar. It hugged my curves, and the royal blue color set off my eyes. It was probably the sexiest dress I'd ever owned, and one that I probably wouldn't ever wear in the general public. We'd been told that we'd have a private room in the restaurant, which meant it was the perfect place to debut the dress. Here, I'd be seen by a lot of people for a short amount of time.

The people I'd be spending most of my time with weren't ones I'd need to worry about if my dress shifted and revealed my scar. I didn't know if Jenna had told Rylan about it, but he was married to her, and after what she'd been through, I doubted he'd even blink. Besides, the chances he'd be looking in the general direction of my scar were low anyway.

"Have I told you how gorgeous you look tonight?" Jalen's voice was low in my ear as he placed his hand on the small of my back.

"You have." I smiled at him. "And you're not so bad yourself."

He was in a casual suit, one without a tie and the top button of his dress shirt was undone. This was the sort of place where the people who could afford to rent a private room also received discretion and the bending of some rules. Rules like the one that had every other man in the place wearing a tie.

The hostess gave us both the same polite smile, not lingering on one of us longer than the other, and when we followed her into the private room, she did the same for Jenna and Rylan. Her professionalism set the last of my nerves to rest, and I was smiling as I sat down at the table.

"This place is amazing," I said as I looked around the sleek, black room.

The color should've made things dreary, but all of the surfaces gleamed, reflecting the soft light that came from the brass fixtures all around the room. The size worked for it too. Big enough to fit half a dozen people in it comfortably, but not so large that a small foursome like ours felt out-of-place. The music was soft

"A friend of mine owns it," Rylan said. "But it deserves its stellar reputation. The food is amazing, and the staff is wonderful."

"He'll even have someone deliver it to us sometimes," Jenna said. She laughed. "The kids prefer pizza though."

"Do you have a regular sitter for them?" I asked.

Rylan chuckled. "It depends on who you ask."

"We usually have Rylan's sister, Suzette, stay with the kids, but sometimes we ask Zeke," Jenna explained with a laugh. "He's one of Rylan's oldest friends, but it's debatable whether or not he's an entirely good influence on our kids."

"Are you looking for someone?" Rylan asked as he leaned back to let the waiter fill his glass of wine. "I never asked if you had kids."

"Just curious," I quickly said. The last thing I needed was Jalen thinking I was hiding a kid or a pregnancy. "No kids."

"Do you want–" Rylan jumped as if something had shocked him...or someone had kicked him. He gave Jenna a surprised look, and she raised an eyebrow. "I wasn't going to ask about kids," he said. "I was just going to ask if they wanted something other than the Cabernet Sauvignon to drink."

Jenna flushed. "Sorry."

He laughed and leaned over to kiss her temple. "Wouldn't be the first time you've kicked me for no reason."

"I always have a reason," she countered. "My reasons just aren't always right."

Rylan glanced at Jalen and me. "You two are my witnesses. She admitted that she's not always right."

I held up my hands. "I heard nothing."

We all looked at Jalen, who shook his head. "Oh, no. I'm not getting involved in this. There's no good answer."

"It's a good thing you're not looking for a babysitter," Rylan said, steering us back a bit. "I wouldn't recommend

Suzette to anyone with small children. She tried babysitting once when she was fifteen, and she hasn't touched a kid since. Diana and Jeremiah are pretty much her only exceptions."

"What happened?" I asked.

"Let's just say it involved projectile vomiting and an attempt to flush her coat down the toilet."

"Yikes," I said as we all laughed.

I'd never really given much thought to having kids. I'd seen how hard being a single parent had been on Anton, and I knew he'd never regretted taking me in or resented me for a change in his life that he hadn't asked for. I would never intentionally become a single parent. It might be great for other people, but I couldn't handle it. Since I'd never let myself think about marriage, the kid question hadn't really come up.

Besides, it wasn't like I had the best example of a family to fall back on. I'd be worried I'd fuck a kid up if they had to rely on me for anything.

It really said something about Jenna's strength and determination that she had two kids, especially since talking about the things they'd gone through would probably trigger memories of her own past. She and Rylan were amazing people, and for the first time in a long time, I liked the idea of having friends. Of having *them* for friends.

The conversation became little snippets here and there as we focused on our food.

I'd gotten the sea bass, and the first bite was divine. I didn't eat fish often because I'd never learned to prepare it myself and I rarely wanted to trust a chef I didn't know.

Rylan's and Jenna's praise had prompted my order, and I was glad that I could give a positive report.

This was nice, being here with them. I didn't need to worry about hiding my past or worrying that they'd see right through me. I could be myself. If I mentioned my father being in prison, it wouldn't silence the room. I could talk about my mother without being afraid of the questions that would come. If they did ask questions, they wouldn't be offended if I didn't answer.

I felt the prick of tears and took a slow breath to steady myself. After everything that had gone on these past few weeks, my emotions were closer to the surface than they'd ever been. At least these would be good tears. I'd never had much occasion for those in my life.

Jalen put his hand on my knee and gave a gentle squeeze. When I looked at him, his expression was soft. "You okay?" It was barely a whisper, and I appreciated him trying to keep the question private.

"I'm great," I said, giving him a smile.

"Jalen, I have a business-related question for you," Rylan interrupted the moment.

"I thought we agreed no business tonight," Jenna said.

"Just one question." He gave Jenna an impossibly charming smile. "I promise it'll only be one and then I'll be good the rest of the night."

"Doubtful," she said. The love shining in her eyes took away any bite their banter might have had.

"Thanks." Rylan turned to Jalen. "Do you have any experience with the latest software update for the Guardian security system? I'm thinking about upgrading

Archer Enterprises, but I've heard some people say that it's not all it's promised to be."

Jalen nodded. "I've heard that too. They wanted me to look at their specs before they went to market, but they refused to give me consultant credit because they didn't want people thinking that my company was involved in the production."

Jenna sighed and looked over at me, shaking her head. "We've lost them. Once he gets talking tech, it's all over. I bet Jalen's the same way."

I didn't tell her that I didn't know Jalen well enough to know if that was his tendency or not. Maybe, in a few months, I'd be able to contribute something to the conversation. Right now, I just laughed and let myself enjoy the rest of the evening. The future would get here when it got here.

FOURTEEN

Going incognito in November was easier than it would have been in the summer. It'd started snowing sometime before dawn, a dry sort of snow that whipped across my skin with an almost brutal wind. In a way, I was thankful for it though. It meant I was able to bundle myself up with a coat, hat, and scarf, and not look out of place at all. It also meant that people weren't going to be paying much attention to whether or not they were being followed.

The downside, however, was that I knew it would be difficult to recognize my target if she was bundled up like me. If she even left the office today. It would be just my luck if this snow turned into a storm and kept Jessica Lee inside for weeks.

As it grew closer to lunchtime, I decided to take a risk. I bundled back up and got out of my car. The doctor Jessica worked for was a general practitioner, which meant I could probably slip inside unobtrusively and watch when

Jessica left. It was risky, but my choices were on the limited side. I had no way of knowing if I'd be able to spot her, which meant I could spend hours in my car or pacing outside, wasting time.

I hadn't taken that into consideration when I'd decided to take this case. I didn't really have a problem with infidelity cases but working with Jenna had given me a taste of being part of something bigger, and it was that thought that kept nagging at me.

"Focus," I muttered as I bent my head against the wind. "Solve the case, move on to the next one."

When I opened the door, the gust of warm air made me sigh. I always needed a few days to make the adjustment between seasons. By next week, I wouldn't notice the cold until we were under three feet of snow.

Snow in the mountains. I had to admit, I was looking forward to it. It'd be beautiful.

As I stepped through the second set of doors, I saw Jessica right away. She looked up from where she was working at her computer, and I nodded at her without taking off my hat or scarf.

"Can I help you, hon?" She had a slight Southern accent, making me wonder where she'd moved from.

"Just waiting for someone." The scarf muffled my voice, but I counted that as a positive thing. I went over to a seat across from her desk and picked up a magazine. I figured I'd have about ten minutes before I started looking suspicious for not taking off my hat and coat.

Fortunately, I'd only been there for six minutes when she stood up and announced that she was taking an early lunch. I waited until she left to get up. I forced myself not to rush as I pulled my phone out of my pocket and looked at it. The worst thing a person could do when doing something like this was overreact. I needed to pretend that I really had just gotten a message from someone.

By the time I was outside again, I worried that I'd moved too slow, but then I saw a familiar hot pink coat a few feet away. I started after her, my phone still out. If she looked behind her, she'd hopefully just see someone engrossed in her phone.

I kept glancing around as we went, trying to figure out where she was going. We'd bypassed the parking lot to the office, and she didn't seem to be stopping at any of the cars on the street either. The wind was dying down, but I couldn't see her wanting to go anywhere that would necessitate a long walk, especially with that teased hairdo.

She paused, and I went a couple more steps before I slowed, frowning at my phone as if I was looking at something important. She looked around, and I sighed. She was attempting to be stealthy and was really bad at it. Which meant she was either about to go on a shopping spree...or she was meeting someone in secret.

When she walked into the Holiday Inn, I knew which it was about to be. My background check on Evan had come back with exactly what he'd said I'd find. Which meant she probably wasn't cheating on him because he was abusive. I understood how some women couldn't leave their abusers, but if she just didn't want to be with him anymore, she should just walk out instead of just sneaking around. But, hey, it was her choice to make.

I followed her into the lobby, lingering by the door and rubbing my hands together to warm them. I kept track of her via her reflection, then made my way up to the counter.

"How can I help you?" The kid behind the desk barely looked old enough to be out of high school.

I pulled off my hat and scarf, giving him a warm smile. "I'd really like to know what room my friend just rented."

"Your friend?" He sounded skeptical but didn't threaten to kick me out, so I'd take it.

I let my smile fade and my bottom lip tremble. "I thought she was my friend, but now I think she's meeting my husband. It'll just kill me if he's cheating on me, especially with her."

He leaned across the counter, a concerned look on his face. "She's not sleeping with your husband."

I sniffled. "How do you know?"

"Because she's meeting a woman."

Oh.

I hadn't seen that coming.

Now what?

I made a silent apology to the kid and then scowled at him. Eyes narrowed, I hardened my voice. "How do I know you're not lying? He could've paid you to tell me that. Or she could have."

He looked a little freaked out. "No one paid me anything, ma'am."

I pointed at him, honestly a little annoyed at the *ma'am*. "Then you're lying to get me out of here. Just let me see for myself, and then I'll go, I promise. Give me a key, and I'll pretend that I stole it. I'll open the door and see for myself, and then I'll leave. I promise."

I let a hysterical edge creep into the last couple words and watched the panic fill his face.

"Okay, okay!" He grabbed a keycard and shoved it across the desk.

"Thank you." I sniffled again and headed for the elevator, unable to believe that shit had worked.

Mrs. Lee was on the second floor, and I doubted she'd have her curtains pulled back so my best chance at getting a picture of her in a compromising position would be when I opened the door. A picture would be nearly impossible. A video, however...

I took out my phone and quickly set it up before using my scarf to hold it in place. It wasn't the most secure or practical thing, but it'd work for what I needed it to do.

I waited until I got right to the door before starting the phone recording. Then I swiped the card and pushed the door open, an accusation already on my lips.

"Roger, you dirty, rotten, bast–"

The last of my doubt regarding the desk clerk's truthfulness disappeared as Jessica Lee looked up from where she'd had her face buried between a brunette's legs only seconds before.

That hadn't taken them long.

The brunette pushed her skirt down as she sat up. "Excuse me?"

Jessica flushed, wiping at her mouth with her hands. "You were at the doctor's office."

"I'm so sorry," I stammered. "I thought my husband, Roger...I think he's cheating on me..."

I held up my hand and slowly backed out of the room. As I pulled the door shut, I heard them talking.

"Jess, it's okay."

"Moira, what if Evan knows?"

"You heard her. She thought her husband was cheating. Besides, we both know Evan's too stupid to think either of us are stepping out on him."

Either of them?

I frowned as I turned off the video, and I was still frowning when I handed back the keycard. The clerk asked me something, but I ignored him. I had my footage, but I wouldn't consider my job finished until I knew who the brunette was, and how they were *both* connected to Evan.

I needed to think on things for a while. My stomach growled, and I looked at my phone. It was closing in on noon, and lunch sounded good. If I got something and took it back to the office to eat, I wouldn't be able to stop myself from chewing over the problem. Eventually, I needed to get there, but I needed a break from it first.

Maybe I could get some company for lunch.

I looked up at the street signs. I'd spent a little time in this part of the city, and if I remembered correctly, Sylph Industries was only a couple blocks away. Jalen usually took his lunch about now.

I decided to drive over, and by the time I got there, I was looking forward to a nice meal and good conversation.

We hadn't made any plans for the weekend, so maybe that would be something we'd talk about.

I stepped into the lobby and heard him before I saw him.

"Thank you for coming."

I turned toward his voice, preparing a snarky comment for his odd statement. The words died in my mouth as I saw he wasn't talking to me. He was focused on a too-familiar figure who already had her hand on his arm.

Elise.

I wasn't going to jump to conclusions, but I wasn't going to cause a scene here either. When we talked about this, we'd do it privately. Besides, I refused to give Elise the satisfaction of knowing how much I hated seeing her with Jalen. And no matter how much it pissed me off, I would trust him to tell me when he was ready.

FIFTEEN

THE BRUNETTE WAS MOIRA CAGE. IT HADN'T TAKEN me long to find her. I'd picked up lunch and gone back to my office to do some research. Less than an hour later, I found her on the website for Evan Lee's car dealership. She was standing next to him, smiling, and Evan was standing far too close to her. If I had to bet that his hand was on her ass, I was fairly certain I'd win.

Now, whether that meant that Evan was being overly flirtatious or that the two of them had been involved, I didn't know, but that wasn't what I'd been hired to find. Once I had a name, I compressed the video file I'd loaded onto my computer, attached it to an email that included a summary of what I'd learned, and then sent it off to Evan.

I was glad I'd asked him for his email address. Even though I had caught Jessica cheating, it didn't mean I wanted Evan in my office again. The less I had to talk to him, the better. Considering how he'd leered at me before, I didn't want to give him an opportunity to do it again.

After I sent the email, I went back to Jenna's case. She hadn't given me anything new to look at on the trafficking cases, and today wasn't a good day to try for new photos of the addresses I'd already obtained. The weather was too bad to get anything clear. Jenna's personal case, however, had tons of work to be done.

For a few hours, I managed to lose myself in research and planning, stopping only when my phone buzzed with a text from Jalen.

Want some dinner? I don't feel like eating alone tonight.

Well, at least he didn't say 'we need to talk,' and I'd take that as a good thing. Maybe he wanted to talk to me about meeting with Elise, or he truly just didn't want to eat alone. Either way, I knew once I sent him a response, he was coming to see me, not going to see her.

And I refused to let my mutinous mind tell me any differently.

To prevent myself from overthinking, I went home, took a shower, and picked up a few things until he showed up with pizza, breadsticks, and a side of wings.

"Hey," he said as I opened the door. "You look nice."

I was wearing a pair of comfy jeans and a long-sleeved cotton t-shirt, both of which were clean and presentable, but nothing special. Score one for Jalen. When I saw that he'd gotten one of those pizzas with all the different kinds of cheeses, I awarded him another point.

"What do you want to drink?" I asked as he followed me into the kitchen. "I pretty much have water, orange juice, and alcohol."

He laughed, the warm sound slithering over every inch of me. "Whatever you're having."

It was probably a good thing that I didn't have any hard liquor here because the way my nerves were going, I could've used a shot or three. I reached into my fridge and pulled out two beers. I didn't drink it a lot, but it was the perfect complement to pizza, in my opinion.

We went into the living room, and I turned the volume down on the TV rather than turning it off. Pauses in our conversation would feel less awkward if there was some background noise, and I was uncertain enough about where things stood with us to want to plan for those possible uncomfortable moments.

After we'd both settled on the couch and served ourselves, I waited to see where he took things first.

"I'm glad you wanted to share dinner," he said. "I really needed to see a friendly face after the day I've had."

That sounded promising, but I tried to keep that thought from showing on my face. "Things didn't go well?"

He shook his head as he chewed. He took a long drink, then explained, "First, I had three programmers call in sick with that nasty flu bug that's going around, and of course, they're the ones doing a lot of the base coding, so other programmers can't do their work. Then, I get a call from Elise, saying she wants to talk about signing our divorce papers, finally. So, I ask her to come to the office."

I went still for several long seconds, then forced myself to pick up my beer and take a drink.

"But, when she gets there, all she wants to do is talk about how we can't throw away all this history we have."

He scowled at his pizza. "Still, I had lunch with her, thinking I could maybe get through to her. She wanted to talk about it instead of pretending I'd never filed, and that was a step in the right direction."

Another long drink of beer on his part while I took another bite of pizza I could barely taste.

"We spent an hour together and accomplished absolutely nothing." He shook his head. "I should have told her that I wouldn't talk to her again unless we sat down with our lawyers."

"Do you think she'd actually agree to that?"

He shrugged. "Probably not, but at least I would've been able to eat my lunch in peace, and considering how my afternoon went, I could've used the break. As soon as I got back to the office, I find out that one of my techs, Matt, has just discovered a huge problem with a program that I'd thought would be ready for release next week. So I spent my afternoon trying to figure out who I could pull off of other projects to fix something that should've been taken care of weeks ago, and I can't even blame anyone else because I completely missed it too."

He sounded so frustrated that I felt guilty for even considering that he might've been hiding Elise from me. I was even more glad now that I'd walked away and given him the benefit of the doubt.

"How was your day?" he asked.

Instead of telling him that I'd closed a case where I was pretty sure that the client's wife was cheating on him with his mistress, I leaned over and kissed his cheek.

"What was that for?" He gave me a puzzled smile.

"Not that I'll ever complain about a kiss from you. I'm just not sure what prompted it."

I set down my empty plate and took his plate from him as I slid closer. His leg was a solid presence against mine, and I reflected for a moment about how much that described what he'd become to me. A solid presence. Someone I could count on. Since he'd come to me in Indiana to apologize for flaking out on me, he hadn't made the same mistake. He'd faced the trial head-on, tried to protect me from Elise, wanted to share his day with me.

This time, when I moved toward him, it was to press my mouth against his, to show him all the things I wasn't quite ready to say. Including that *l*-word that kept creeping into my mind at the most unexpected moments. I wasn't there yet, but it was coming.

I pushed away all thoughts of the future and what it might or might not hold. I wanted to be about now.

He caught me around the waist as he angled my head to deepen the kiss. Without knowing exactly when it had happened, he'd taken over things, but I was glad to relinquish control to him. His fingers flexed against my spine, the pressure as reassuring as it was erotic. It amazed me how he was able to make me feel both out of control and safe at the same time.

He made an urgent sound in the back of his throat and pulled me onto his lap. I put my knees on either side of his hips and wished I'd put on a skirt. It would've been so easy to have him inside me. Unzip his pants, pull out his cock, sink down onto him. Three simple steps to satisfy the deep ache growing between my legs.

I put my hands on his cheeks, relishing in the stubble scratching my palms. I had the sudden urge to push back and beg him to go down on me just so I could feel the whisker-burn on the insides of my thighs. I'd gotten over a lot of my self-consciousness when it came to my body, but I still struggled with thinking about it too much.

He pulled back and caught my chin in a firm grip. "I swear, sometimes, I can hear you thinking."

He took my mouth with a deep, bruising kiss. His teeth latched onto my bottom lip, and he worried at it until it was swollen and throbbing. I'd read books where the author had described lips as being 'bee-stung' and I had a feeling that's what I'd see if I looked into a mirror.

"Talk to me," he said. "Tell me what's going on in that head of yours." I flushed, and the response made him chuckle. "That bad?"

The hand on my back slid under my shirt, leaving a hot trail up my spine to my bra. His talented fingers made short work of the clasp.

"Is there something you wanted me to do that I'm not doing?" He sounded intrigued. "You can ask me anything, Rona, and I won't think of you differently because of it."

"It's not *bad*," I said. "I just surprise myself sometimes, with the things that I want."

He considered that for a minute while he pulled off my shirt and bra. As the cool air hit my skin, my nipples pebbled, tightening into hard little points.

"Maybe I should tell you some of the things that go on in my head." He flicked the tip of his tongue against one nipple, then the other. "I'm still planning on fucking your ass. I also want to do it at least once while I have a nice, thick dildo in your pussy. I want you to feel what it's like to be completely filled, but I won't ever share you with someone."

My entire body clenched at his words, but I wasn't sure if I was more turned on by what he wanted to do with me or by his declaration that he'd never share me. I'd never had anyone want to be possessive with me.

"I have this fantasy about fucking you in public." He rolled one of my nipples between his thumb and forefinger, not attempting to even try to be gentle. "Outside somewhere maybe. Take you on a hike and then step off the trail. Lean you against a tree, tug down your pants, and fuck you right there."

Damn. If he kept this up, I was going to come right here.

I tugged on his shirt, and he leaned forward to let me pull it off. I ran my hands across his shoulders, his chest, smiling as his muscles twitched and bunched. "I was thinking how I want you to go down on me so I can feel that five o'clock shadow on the insides of my thighs."

His eyes darkened. "Take off your pants and underwear."

I climbed off him, my hands shaking as I hurried to follow his instructions. He shifted on the couch, turning until he was laying on his back, his legs bent at the knees to allow him to fit.

"Come here."

I moved up to the end of the couch, taking the hand he offered. With his help, I managed to get back onto the couch, and then I let him position me with my knees on either side of his head, my pussy above his face. A hot flush made its way across my skin, but I didn't complain. When I'd imagined this, we hadn't exactly been in this particular position, but this was somehow hotter.

He put his hands on my hips as he rubbed his cheeks against my skin, giving me a hint of that hot near-pain that I'd craved.

"Ride my face."

A shiver went through me as I looked down at him.

He squeezed my ass. "Come on, babe. Don't tell me you haven't thought about it. Me underneath you. You in control. Deciding how deep I go, where I touch. Where I...lick."

My face burned, but the embarrassment of this particular position wasn't as strong as my desire for what he offered. I nodded, and he eased me forward, then down. I muttered a curse as his tongue teased me. It worked its way between my lips, and I shifted, wanting his tongue in a better place. A more *sensitive* place.

He chuckled, and the vibrations made me moan. His head barely moved, but even the most minute of movements made the scruff on his skin abrade the insides of my thighs again. It felt even better than I'd imagined.

The combination of the soft, wet caress of his tongue and the coarse abrasion of his face had my entire body tingling. It was a blistering, tight spiral like nothing I'd ever felt before. A single finger slipped between my cheeks, and a moment later, I felt it press against my anus. The burn spread quickly as the tip breached that ring of muscle, and the moment it hit the knot of pressure inside me, I exploded.

"Yes! Fuck, J!" I squeezed my eyes closed, and I still saw sparks.

I ground down on his face, and his hands held me there, his mouth keeping me on that plateau until it became too much, and I began to beg him to stop. I tried to move away, but now he was in control. A single word could get him to stop, but I hadn't quite reached that point yet. Still, it was torture. Pure ecstasy, but torture nonetheless.

Then his mouth was gone, and he was flipping us over, stretching his long, hard body over mine. At some point, he'd dealt with his own clothing because it was bare skin against bare skin now. I hardly had enough time to process the sensations before he buried himself inside me.

I cried out as that thick, hard shaft split me in two. His mouth crashed down on mine, his tongue delving into my mouth, languidly exploring as he reached down and stroked my clit a few times, making my muscles spasm around his cock.

"Fuck, baby," he groaned, his mouth moving down my jaw and throat as he spoke, "You feel so good."

He pressed his face against the side of my neck and rocked against me, creating perfect friction that made my entire body shudder. He pulled my leg up straight, my calf resting on his chest, my ankle on his shoulder. The stretch and burn down the back of my thigh mingled with the building heat inside me. I waited for him to drive into me hard and fast, but he didn't.

He pulled back until just the tip remained, then eased

forward, his pace leisurely, but deep. He reached every inch of me, filled every part in ways that I'd only ever felt with him.

That fire low in my belly flared, then dimmed, smoldering before roaring to life, each change brought about by a new stroke or bite. His hands moved over my body, cupping my breasts, tugging on my nipples. It was gentle and rough. Hard and soft. A dichotomy of sensation.

"Come for me, pretty girl," he murmured. His breath ghosted across my skin, and I shivered. "I want that tight pussy of yours to squeeze me, milk out every last drop of my cum."

"I need more," I whimpered. I was so close. I could feel my body ready to shatter, but I couldn't quite get there.

"More what, baby?" He scraped his teeth on my collarbone, then bit my shoulder. "Tell me. What more do you want?"

I shook my head. "I don't know. I don't know. I just need...I need...please, J. I need..." I grabbed his arm, digging my nails into his flesh. "J."

My leg dropped as he went up on his knees. He took me with him, forcing my torso up, my weight resting on my shoulders. His eyes locked with mine as he gripped my hips.

"Play with your clit, baby," he said. "Because I'm going to fuck you until I come, and if you don't come by then, you get to wait until I'm ready to go again."

I wanted to ask him if he'd punish me, and I wanted to tell him that I could get myself off on my own. The look in his eyes told me neither would be appreciated. A little thrill went through me at the knowledge that I could affect him like that. I watched my hand slide up toward him, toward that place where our bodies came together.

My fingers moved through the thin layer of curls, gathering moisture. The first pass over my clit had me gasping. It was swollen, sensitive, throbbing...fuck...

"That's it, baby," he said. "Come on my cock."

Now it was time for hard and fast.

Neither of us lasted long. Half a dozen strokes and I came with a scream. My body stiffened, and Jalen cursed. My fingers pressed tight against my clit, sending a nearly-painful rush of pleasure through me, and I came again before the first climax finished.

He pulled out suddenly, his fist moving over his swollen cock until he finished, his cum decorating my stomach. He collapsed half on top of me, pulling me close.

At some point, I'd need to clean my couch, I realized. But right now, I was content where I was.

SIXTEEN

Rocks dug into my hands and arms. Cutting. Bleeding. I tried to push myself to my feet again, but everything was slippery and wet. Hot wet.

The thick scent of iron and copper coated my tongue, the inside of my nose.

I started to push my knees underneath me, and I screamed. Pain like nothing I'd ever felt before ripped through me. I pressed my hands to my stomach and something squished between my fingers.

It was slimy and bloody and wasn't supposed to be outside my body.

I didn't want to know what that was.

Someone screamed, and it wasn't me. A child. Two children. Both screaming. The sound went straight through my head. Stabbing stabbing stabbing...

Why wasn't someone shutting them up?

I knew the answer to the question, but I didn't want to

think about it too hard. I didn't want to know. But I knew. I knew. I knew.

Crunch, crunch, crunching...

Someone was walking toward me on the gravel. I was on my stomach, all those inside parts mixing with the dirt and stones in the driveway.

"Stupid girl." Daddy grabbed my hair and yanked my head up. "I always hated you."

"No, no. You didn't. You loved me before the accident took you away." My neck was hurting now, and I didn't know why I could feel it over the pain from where I was torn apart. "You did."

"I didn't," he said. "I pretended to want a sniveling little brat like you so your mom would stop bitching. I would've rather had a boy. Someone I could teach things to. Instead, I got you. I hate you. I wish I would've killed you along with your whore mother."

"No!" I screamed at him. "No! That's not true! You loved us once!"

"Never." He twisted his hand in my hair. "I didn't want you, and I didn't want the new bastard she tried to convince me was mine."

New bastard.

He'd killed them both.

Killed them.

Killed me.

Killed–

I jerked awake, my heart racing. I flipped on my light as I pushed myself up. I bent my knees and wrapped my arms around them. I'd had dozens of different nightmares over the years, but these were the ones that shook me the most.

Most people assumed that when a victim of a violent crime had nightmares, they were about the event itself or about the person who'd hurt us. I'd read accounts of people who'd lost loved ones in sudden, violent ways, and they often said that the worst dreams were the ones where their loved one was still alive. Weddings that would never happen. Grandchildren they'd never see.

For me, there were two types. The nightmares where my father told me that he'd never loved me, that the good memories I had were lies. The others were the dreams where my father had never been hurt, and that we were a family. My parents, me...and the baby she'd been six weeks pregnant with when she died.

Then there were the ones that were both, ones like tonight.

I hadn't known about the baby at the time and hadn't learned about him or her until many years had passed. Shortly after Anton's death, I'd been cleaning up some of his things when I found a shoebox of items I'd never seen before.

Some had been things I hadn't recognize, but I'd assumed they'd been important to him. There'd also been pictures of him and my mom, programs from graduations and funerals. Pressed flowers. Ticket stubs from more than half a dozen Broadway shows. *Rent*, *Wicked*, *Phantom of the Opera*. We'd gone to those three together. I didn't know who he'd taken to the other ones.

And then I'd seen an envelope with my name on it.

Inside had been clippings from a dozen or so news outlets, all the stories about my family. More than one of them had mentioned that my mother had been pregnant when she was murdered. One had an interview with a friend of hers that had shed some light on things.

My mom had been scared to tell my father about the baby. Apparently, he'd been accusing her of cheating on him on and off for months.

I couldn't keep thinking about this, or it'd drive me crazy. Whenever I had a dream like this, I had to get up and get moving, find something to take my mind off the nightmare that had been my life.

Fortunately, I'd neglected enough basic housework that I'd be able to stay busy for a few hours. After that, I'd see where things stood.

I was halfway through washing up some dishes when my phone rang. My heart jumped, and I barely took the time to dry my hands before I grabbed it.

"Hello?"

The moment the robotic recording started up again, I cursed. It took all the restraint I possessed to set my phone down instead of throwing it against a wall.

That was it. I was done ignoring the issue and hoping it would go away. I needed my father to stop calling me. Blocking the number wouldn't do any good. Unlike most people, I still had a landline. Ever since that night, I'd been terrified of being in a position where I needed help and couldn't get it. Having a landline made me feel safer because it gave me two different ways to call out. If one wasn't working, the other could still possibly work.

I could try talking to someone at the prison, but I doubted they'd restrict outgoing phone calls without a real reason, maybe not without a court order. Since I'd never let it get to the point of actually talking to him, I couldn't claim he was threatening me. I had no clue why he was calling. It could've been to threaten me. Or yell at me. Or a dozen other reasons I couldn't think of right now.

If I called the prison, I'd simply be a daughter not wanting to speak with her incarcerated father. Unless, of course, I wanted to explain that the reason I didn't want to talk to my father was because I was one of his victims.

I needed someone else to reach out for me. I hated asking for help, but I hated more the sick feeling in my stomach when I thought of how many times I was going to hear the phone ring and wonder if it was him. I'd spent too much of my life dealing with the consequences of what happened that day. I finally felt like I was moving past it, and I couldn't let his persistence change that.

Clay.

Clay worked at the FBI. He could contact the prison or whoever he needed to talk to, use his position. Even though the FBI had no jurisdiction over things like this, he could make it a personal favor.

I needed to talk to him.

Today.

———

"I'LL MAKE some calls this afternoon," Clay promised.

"You don't have to rush," I said as I set down what was

left of my chicken sandwich. "Whenever you have the time."

"I'm not letting that...*man* take one more moment of your life from you," he insisted. His tone was even, but there was no hiding the fury in his eyes. "In fact, no more talking about him. Tell me about how things are going at Burkart Investigations."

The knot in my stomach loosened, and I smiled. Clay would take care of things for me like the good friend he was, and I'd be able to focus on the rest of my life.

SEVENTEEN

"This is delicious," I said as I pulled my feet up under me. "I think I might want you to cook for us all the time now."

Jalen grinned at me as he served himself a second helping of the pasta he'd made. "Then it's a good thing you like this because there's really not much more I know how to make, and none of it well."

I sighed. "I suppose it was too good to be true."

He leaned over, fork poised to steal. I scowled at him and pulled my plate closer to my chest. "Try it, buddy, and find out what it feels like to get stabbed with a fork."

He held up his hands, laughing. "It's all yours." He leaned back but reached over and put his hand on my knee. "Do you want to take some home with you to have tomorrow?"

I shook my head. "No, thank you. I have leftovers from my lunch yesterday."

"What'd you have?"

"A chicken sandwich," I said as I ate the last of my cheese-stuffed ravioli. "But Clay gave me the rest of his turkey on rye, so I had that last night for dinner."

"You had lunch with Clay yesterday?" Jalen's voice sounded flat.

I hurried to explain. "My dad called me again yesterday morning, and I finally just had enough. Clay's going to help me get the calls to stop."

Jalen stood suddenly. He picked up his plate and mine, then headed into the kitchen. I frowned at the abrupt behavior. Was he seriously annoyed that I'd had lunch with Clay? Okay, I hadn't called him to tell him yesterday because, by the time I'd gotten home, my mind had been focused on planning out this upcoming week's schedule.

When he didn't come back after a couple minutes, I went after him. He was cleaning up but didn't look at me when I came in, making me think that he was doing something for the sake of movement, not because it actually needed to be done.

"Are you mad that I had lunch with Clay? You know he and I are friends. That means I'm going to see him from time to time." No response. "I didn't give you the silent treatment when you had lunch with Elise. Yes, it took me longer to tell you, but I'd started thinking about stuff on the way home and–"

"Have you changed your mind?" he interrupted quietly. "Do you want to be with Clay?"

"No!" I snapped. "He's my friend, and I think it's pretty shitty to be mad at me when you spent time with your *wife,* and I didn't complain."

He spun around, eyes flashing. "You think I'm upset because you had lunch with Clay? Dammit, Rona! I'm not that petty! I'm pissed because you went to him when you were upset, and you didn't even think to tell me you were hurting."

"Because Clay can do something about it." What the hell was his issue? "I didn't come to you to stop my dad's calls because Clay has the contacts needed to make something happen."

Jalen tossed the dish towel onto the counter. "No, I get that part. That's logical. What's bothering me is that you didn't call me to tell me what happened and where you were going."

"I don't need to check in with you about everything." I cross my arms. My cheeks were hot, my heart racing.

"Not check in," he said, his voice tight. "Don't you get it? I want to know about stuff like this because I care about you. I want to know what's going on in your life. I want to be the one to talk through things with you." He reached out and touched my arm. "I want you to lean on me and let me take care of you."

Well, damn. I felt like a piece of shit now.

"Yes, I'm angry, but it's because I'm hurt." His hand slid up my arm, over my shoulder, and then his fingers curled around the back of my neck. His thumb strummed over the pulse point under my jaw. "I thought we were going to be more to each other."

"I'm sorry," I said quietly. "It was wrong of me to go to Clay instead of you."

"You're right that he has the connections you need to

get this taken care of," Jalen said. He brushed his lips across mine in a ghost of a kiss. "I just want to know what you're going through because I want to be there for you. Even if I can't be the one rescuing you."

I raised an eyebrow. "*Rescuing me?*" I echoed.

He grinned. "Come on, who doesn't want to be rescued by a handsome white knight?"

I leaned into him, wrapping my arms around his neck. "How about *you* be the damsel in distress, and *I'll* be the beautiful white knight?"

"I'll bet you look hot in body armor."

I was still laughing when his mouth covered mine.

EIGHTEEN

I'd been grinning like an idiot all morning, and it was Jalen's fault. After we made up, we'd spent the rest of the day together. It had started snowing not long after lunch, but it'd been one of those beautiful snowy days. Cold, but not bitterly so. Not a lot of wind. We'd bundled up and gone for a walk, then back to his place where we'd made hot cocoa and snuggled on the couch while binge-watching a vampire comedy series.

Topping it all off, he'd texted me this morning.

Do you have any plans for Thanksgiving? Rylan and Jenna invited me over, and I'd love for you to come with me. Or we can do our own thing. I just want to spend the holiday with the person I'm most thankful for.

I loved the invitation, and I accepted, whether we went to the Archers' place or spent the day as just the two of us. It was his reasoning that had my stomach doing flips.

He was most thankful for me.

Handsome, intelligent billionaire Jalen Larsen was most thankful for *me*.

It didn't seem possible.

I heard the bell I'd installed above the front door ring, and I pulled my focus back to my job. I could think about Jalen later.

"Come on back," I called. "I'm sorry, I don't have a receptionist yet."

I straightened in my seat and opened my mouth to greet my prospective client...and froze as Evan Lee stormed into the office.

"Fucking bitch!"

As he continued to curse and pace, I stared at him, completely caught off-guard. I didn't know how to handle this. He hadn't threatened me, and I wasn't even entirely sure if he was directing his colorful commentary at me, which meant I didn't know if I was in danger. If I called the cops on him, I could end up ruining the reputation Adare had worked so hard to cultivate. If I tried to throw him out myself, I might be able to take him, but that might also be an insanely bad idea.

Shit. I really needed to get a second person in here.

"Mr. Lee." I finally managed to get my voice back, and the words came out stronger than I'd hoped. "Mr. Lee, can I help you?"

He spun around and stalked toward me until I could smell the alcohol coming off him in waves. "Where are they?"

"Where are who?"

"Don't play stupid with me! You followed them. You have to know where they are."

"Your wife?"

He put his hands on my desk and leaned toward me. "Yes. My fucking wife and my fucking girlfriend who've been fucking behind my back!"

"I sent you all the information I found," I said, keeping my voice low and even. "The only place I ever saw them was at the hotel, and I doubt they went back there. Are you sure they're both gone?"

"You sent me that fucking video, and it's all I can think about. I close my eyes, and I see my fucking wife with her face in my girlfriend's twat."

Wasn't that charming? Still, I managed to keep a bland expression as he kept ranting.

"I kept waiting for her to come home so I could talk to her about it. Find out what the fuck she was doing. But she never came home. I went to Moira's to see if they were together, but no one was there."

Shit. I was afraid he was actually right. After I caught Jessica and Moira in the hotel, it made sense that they might take off together. Maybe they had something more than a fling. Maybe they were both tired of fucking Evan. Either way, he'd been left out, and he was pissed.

"I think you should go home." I got to my feet but kept the desk between us. "Get some sleep. Let your head clear. Give them both time to come back. They have lives here. They're not going to just up and leave."

Except I thought they might do exactly that. Neither woman had the sort of careers here that couldn't be easily replaced. Moving somewhere else and starting a fresh life wouldn't be difficult for them. Especially if one or both had been smart enough to take some of Evan's money.

His eyes narrowed. "You think they'll be back?"

I didn't want to lie, but I also wasn't going to give him the whole truth. "I think it's a possibility."

"How could they do it?" His shoulders slumped, all his anger seemingly bled away. "I treated them both good."

I was tempted to point out that the fact that he'd been married to one and 'dating' the other made it hard to believe he'd been 'good' to them, but it wasn't my responsibility to make him see any of that. Or any of my business to judge them.

"You'd have to ask them," I said, finally daring to come out from behind the desk. "Which I'm sure you'll be able to do soon. But they won't come looking for you here."

"I'll go home and wait," he announced as if it was a thought that had suddenly occurred to him.

"That's a great idea," I said as I walked him to the door. As soon as he left, I closed the door and locked it, flipping the sign over to closed. If Evan saw it, he might be insulted, but I didn't care at the moment. I needed a few minutes after that chaos.

I'd barely had a single minute before my phone rang, and I took a step toward the office before I realized it was my cell and not the one that belonged to the company.

Jenna's name appeared on the screen when I pulled it from my pocket. "Jenna?"

"Are you busy?"

"Is something wrong?" I asked, suddenly worried.

After the way my past had come back to bite me in the ass, I hadn't been able to stop thinking about what would happen if my investigations into Jenna's family brought her past into her present. I'd never forgive myself if I was responsible for bringing up all those awful things again.

"I just got off the phone with Agent Matthews," she said. "Unofficially, of course. He gave me some information that needs...expanded."

Expanded.

She didn't need to spell it out for me. There were things that the FBI couldn't do. Things that weren't always illegal, though they sometimes were just that. Jenna and I didn't need search warrants or supporting evidence. Sure, the thought of violating people's rights wasn't one that sat easily with me, but even when I'd been with the FBI, I'd struggled with the idea of a possible criminal's rights being more important than that of a victim. It was like Jenna had said before, how she couldn't understand how her mother's right to continue having children to abuse superseded the rights of those children.

I understood the reasons behind innocent until proven guilty, behind the laws that protected the rights of citizens. That it was better for a guilty person to go free than an innocent person go to jail.

In instances like this, however, I had a difficult time with the justice system.

"I'll be right there."

NINETEEN

I kept my pace even as I made my way down the sidewalk. The weather had cleared, which meant it was cold but sunny. The perfect excuse to wear sunglasses with my hat and scarf. If I went inside, I'd have to take at least the sunglasses off, but I didn't look too out-of-place with them on out here. Some people probably thought I was doing a late walk of shame, needing the sunglasses because of a hangover, but it didn't bother me. If the subject matter hadn't been so awful, I would've been enjoying myself.

Agent Matthews had given Jenna a list of names and no instructions as to what he wanted done. According to her, that's how things went with them when he wanted her help but couldn't legally ask her to work on behalf of the FBI. I didn't ask if he was allowed to give her the names. I didn't know how much Clay was involved, and the last thing I needed was something like this to come between us.

Some of the names she'd been given were local, some weren't, so she took the ones on which she'd need to use her considerable hacker skill set and gave me the locals. With the names came very specific instructions regarding my role in the operation. I was to follow the people on my list, see where they went, who they talked to, what their routines were. Anything suspicious, I was supposed to write down and take it back to Jenna who would check it out in the digital world. I was also supposed to record anything else I felt was significant.

I was *not* to talk to them or interfere with them in any way. I'd seen the expression on Jenna's face though when she'd given me that instruction. She would trust my judgment. Unlike the cops, she and I were private citizens. If we saw something going on that wasn't okay – an adult harassing a child, someone being accosted, that sort of thing – we could get involved with the same risks as any other regular person on the street. She'd hired me independently, without any official record as to whether the information was for her, or for someone else. I assumed she'd covered herself within the arrangement she had with Agent Matthews. Considering who her husband was, I was confident that he'd hired the best attorney money could buy to go over any written documentation.

I had to admit, it was nice to know that I didn't have to follow anyone else's protocol as I followed my target into a boutique. I was two feet inside when I realized that this place wasn't merely a boutique. It was a fetishist boutique. While the front of the shop had displayed a few simple yet sexy nightgowns, inside was a whole other world.

Corsets that ranged from covering everything to covering under the breasts down to the bellybutton. High-heeled boots in every style and size imaginable. Skintight pants and skirts of varying length. Assless chaps. Chains. Whips. Ball-gags. Sex toys that made me blush as I considered how they were meant to be used.

I processed it all in seconds but still couldn't find it in me to move. I was frozen to the spot, calling attention to myself in a way that I definitely didn't want to. The cashier gave me a concerned look, and I wondered if she was trying to think of the best way to approach me without being offensive.

I could do this.

I *had* to do this.

Gritting my teeth, I took off my sunglasses and pocketed them. I gave the cashier a smile and started in the same direction as my target had gone. Nothing here was illegal, I reminded myself. Just because some of it was too far in the kinky zone for me to feel comfortable with didn't mean that there was anything wrong with it. Consent was what mattered.

Hence my reason for following thirty-five-year-old warehouse manager Chuck Elmsworth from his little suburban home to Dominque's Boutique. He was suspected of seducing and then blackmailing underage girls into performing on camera with things from shops like this. The biggest problem trying to take down someone like him was that technology had progressed to the point where men like him were doing live and streaming videos that didn't need hard copy storage.

Jenna and I were hoping that some of Elmsworth's customers would be old school enough that they'd want a physical recording. If we could bust him when he made the move to get his merchandise to his customers, that'd be leverage at the very least.

I reminded myself that I wasn't doing anything wrong by being there. I was an adult, and just because it made me uncomfortable didn't mean that I wasn't supposed to be there. Except, it wasn't the fetish stuff that made me uncomfortable, I realized. Once I'd gotten over the surprise of where I was, the things around me didn't bother me at all. Some of them, I didn't get, but hey, to each their own, right?

As long as it was consensual.

And *that* was the problem I was having at the moment.

Good old Chuck was standing in front of some bondage equipment. Handcuffs. Ropes. Silk scarves. Leather straps. Buckled cuffs. Harnesses. Other more complicated things that I had no clue how they worked. Things that I sincerely hoped Jalen never wanted to use with me.

And Chuck stared at them, the front of his pants tenting out as whatever he was picturing turned him on. I really hoped that Agent Matthews was mistaken, and this guy was just thinking about his legal-age girlfriend or wife. Or maybe a boyfriend or husband. As long as they were over eighteen, I didn't care who got Chuck's motor going.

I didn't go down that aisle but instead went to the next one. It contained a liberal number of different types of lubricant. Dozens of flavors. Warming. Edible.

Without meaning to, I flashed back to the times that

Jalen had promised to fuck me in the ass. On impulse, I grabbed a couple tubes.

Just in case I had to follow Chuck to the register, of course. It had nothing to do with the thrill of anticipation that ran down my spine. Whenever Jalen decided that he was ready to take things there, I was sure he'd be prepared.

And that was not the mission.

I needed to focus. I couldn't let myself get distracted, no matter how tempting the distraction.

A shrill ringtone cut through the air for several seconds before being abruptly cut off.

"I thought I told you never to call me," a man whispered. "*I'll* call you."

Unless someone else had appeared in the aisle I'd just passed, it was Chuck on the phone. I stilled, concentrating on Chuck's side of the conversation.

"Yes, yes, I know what I said, and you'll get your...I'll have everything on time, just like I promised." His voice got quieter, but I was close enough to still make out what he was saying. "Three." Pause. "Yes, they'll follow the script."

Script. Fuck.

"No, I can't get another one. Do you have any idea how hard it is to–"

Another one. Whoever was on the other end of the phone wanted more of what I assumed was kids. Doing things that I didn't even want to imagine them doing.

"I'm getting supplies right now." He sighed. "Do you have a preference between whips and crops?"

My stomach lurched, and I tossed the lube toward the

closest shelf. I didn't bother to wait and see if any of them dropped. I needed to get out of there before I did something I regretted. Like throwing up in the middle of the aisle.

Or walking over to Chuck and kicking him right in the balls.

I managed to make it outside without running and then went a few more feet before stopping to catch my breath. When I'd gone into this, I hadn't known exactly what I'd be looking for, but I'd just found it. It wasn't the sort of thing that would hold up in court, but that wasn't my job. Once I got this back to Jenna, she could hack Chuck's phone records and find out who he was talking to.

The people I'd be following as I helped Jenna would be some of the most despicable types of people on the planet, but I wasn't regretting my offer to help her. I'd enjoyed the PI work, but tracking down cheating spouses, while lucrative, wasn't quite as fulfilling as knowing that I was helping the FBI put away human traffickers.

My stomach had settled, which meant it was now time to call Jenna with the information I'd overheard. After that, I'd see if I could find Yvonne Planter at her place of business. According to Jenna, Yvonne was connected to Chuck's venture in some way and possibly had her fingers into some sweatshops too.

I might not have a badge, but I was doing good work.

I smiled. My mom would've been proud.

TWENTY

I was twelve years old the last time I'd had a big Thanksgiving. Dad's accident had happened at the end of summer, and he hadn't been ready for guests by the time the holidays rolled around. It'd been a good thing we hadn't tried since he'd gotten angry in the middle of the meal and started throwing things. At least the memory of the last real Thanksgiving we'd had together was untarnished.

Neither Anton nor I had ever been up to making a Thanksgiving meal, emotionally or in practicality. We'd made our own tradition where we'd gone to this little diner a couple blocks from the loft. It'd been owned by a family of Jehovah Witnesses, so they kept it open over the holidays for people like them who didn't celebrate holidays, and people like my uncle and me who didn't have anywhere else to go.

After Anton's death, I hadn't wanted to celebrate anything. Moving here, I'd hoped I'd be able to find some quiet sort of acceptance to having holidays myself, find traditions that didn't hurt as much as the ones I'd left behind.

I'd never imagined that I'd be spending Thanksgiving in a mansion with my boyfriend, my new friend, her husband, kids, and the rest of their family. It didn't seem possible.

Now, if I could only get the butterflies in my stomach to believe that this was a good thing, I'd be set.

"You look like you're going to pass out," Jalen said as we walked up to the front door. "That, or throw up."

"I'm okay." I wasn't sure if I was trying to convince him or myself.

He chuckled. "I might believe you if you weren't cutting off the blood supply in my arm."

I flushed as I loosened my grip on his arm. "Sorry."

He shook his head and patted my hand. "Don't worry. If we were going to meet my parents, I'd say you had every right to be nervous, but you know the Archers. They're good people."

I gave him what I hoped was a reassured smile. It wasn't Jenna or Rylan who had me worried. It was Rylan's sister and his best friend. I hoped they both would understand that I wasn't trying to force my way into their family. More than that, it was the kids who had me worried. I'd never spent much time around kids, and this seemed like a crash course kind of thing that never ended well.

Then again, I supposed it was better that Rylan and Jenna learn now rather than later that they should never ask me to babysit.

"Relax," Jalen whispered as he knocked on the door.

"I'll get right on that," I muttered.

The door opened before I could say anything else. A tall, slender young woman with short, dark hair beamed up at us. "Hi! You must be Rona and Jalen. I'm Suzette. Come on in."

"We brought wine," Jalen said as he followed me inside.

"That makes you my favorite new person." Suzette winked at him, then at me. "Don't worry, I know he's taken. I just might want to steal him to take my brother's place when Ry's being an ass. Like he's being now."

"Language, Suz," Jenna called from the kitchen.

"It's not like Diana and I haven't heard the word *ass* before." Jeremiah was leaning against the fridge with a sullen expression on his face.

"Language," Rylan said firmly. "Just because you know it doesn't mean you have to use it."

Jeremiah sighed and rolled his eyes, but even I could see how much he admired Rylan. I could only imagine how much work my friends had put into building trust with their children. As much as I knew Jenna's past had influenced her decision to keep working with Agent Matthews, I knew that she saw her work from a mother's perspective now. She was fighting to protect her children and other children...and she was fighting to hurt the people who'd hurt her kids, and other people's kids.

I pushed aside the maudlin thoughts and smiled. This wasn't work time. This was family time, and that was something I hadn't had in so very long.

"Aunt Suzette!" Diana barreled into the brunette's legs. "I need you to fix my hair. Uncle Zeke made a mess of it."

Suzette laughed as she touched the little girl's lop-sided puffballs of hair. "Yes, he did."

As we entered the kitchen, a tall, handsome man sauntered in from the other side. "I warned her that I'm all thumbs when it comes to hair." He smiled at us and reached around Jenna to grab a carrot off a tray. "She should've waited for Alan to get here."

"What time does his parents' flight leave?" Rylan asked.

"Five forty-five," Zeke said. "He texted me a couple minutes ago to say he's on his way."

"Zeke, this is Rona Quick and Jalen Larsen." Jenna smacked Zeke's hand when he tried to steal another carrot. "Don't spoil your appetite."

"You know that will never happen," Rylan said.

"Good point," Jenna said. "Zeke, why don't you and Jeremiah finish setting the table?"

Before Jeremiah could complain, Zeke nudged his shoulder and gestured to the vegetable tray. To my surprise, the kid picked it up and followed Zeke into the dining room.

"Zeke and Rylan earned his trust pretty quickly," Jenna said quietly. "When it comes to men, he goes by first impressions. He tends to be more skeptical of women, always watching for them to turn on him. Diana wants to trust, but she's still waiting for the other shoe to drop."

I nodded, understanding what she wasn't saying. I'd

never do anything to intentionally cause distrust, but I needed to be extra careful around the kids. Even if we never became close, they needed to see I was trustworthy.

At that moment, I realized what I wanted to do with Burkart Investigations. Tomorrow, I'd take a closer look at the books to see where things stood financially and if my idea was even feasible. I needed to hire a receptionist who could keep the office open while I was in the field, and then I needed to find an investigator who'd be able to take on the everyday cases of infidelity and lost pets, that sort of thing.

Once I didn't have to deal with the majority of the paperwork and simple cases, I'd be able to focus most of my time on criminals. I'd work the cases Jenna hired me for, of course, but I'd find other scumbags who needed to be put away. Anonymous tips worked as long as they stayed anonymous. I'd look into pro bono cases too. Ones like Theo and Meka who didn't have someone like Jalen to pay for an investigator.

I'd catch the cases that fell through the cracks.

"You okay?" Jalen asked, his question interrupting my thought process.

I nodded and smiled. "I'm good. It's been a while since I've been around this many people on a holiday. Takes some getting used to."

He reached down and squeezed my hand. "If it gets to be too much, just say the word, and we'll go. You know Jenna and Rylan will understand."

"Thanks."

I appreciated the gesture, but I wasn't going to take

him up on his offer. As conflicted as my emotions were, I genuinely wanted to be there. My relationship with Adare had softened me up, and the closer I grew to Jalen and Jenna, and even Rylan, the more I wanted to be a part of a family.

I'd missed this more than I'd let myself acknowledge.

I moved over to the stove where Rylan was mixing a stick of butter into a bowl of mashed potatoes. "How can I help?"

TWENTY-ONE

My elbows popped as I stretched my arms above my head. I'd been working at my laptop for most of the day, but I'd accomplished a lot. And I'd been able to watch Christmas specials while I did it. A restful day followed by a date with Jalen tonight. That sounded like the perfect way to continue a great holiday weekend.

I'd ultimately decided to close the office and work from home today. Black Friday was important for retailers all over the country, but I doubted anyone would be clamoring to come see a PI today. It wasn't like I was offering some sort of two-for-one discount or something like that. I had a feeling some people might've expected just that if they'd seen I was open today.

It hadn't been until earlier this afternoon that I'd realized how much Adare had been preparing me to take over until I opened the books. As I went through the now familiar process, I remembered how often over the months before she died that she'd had me doing them for her. She'd said it was because she hated working with numbers, and as her employee, I got to do the things she didn't want to do.

Now, I knew it was because she'd wanted me to not only be familiar with the way things were done. She'd also known I'd need to be able to pick up without needing a learning curve.

There had been one thing, however, she had kept from me. I'd known that Burkart Investigations was doing well, but I hadn't realized that she'd invested some of the profits over the years, then cashed them out shortly before she died. The business had a savings account that could keep things running for two years without me taking a single client.

Even as I stared at the numbers, I still couldn't quite believe it. Because of her careful planning, I'd be able to hire a receptionist right away and be able to take my time finding the right investigator. And I could do it all without feeling guilty about taking on pro bono cases.

Adare would've been pleased.

My cell phone rang, and I picked it up without looking at the screen. "Hello?"

"Where is my daughter?" The man's voice was angry, but I could hear the bright thread of panic weaving through his words.

"Who is this?" My question was blunt but necessary. Reacting to the accusation wouldn't do anything but cause an argument.

"Is this Rona Quick?" He sounded uncertain now.

"It is," I said. "May I ask with whom I'm speaking?"

Politer, more formal. Hopefully, it would prompt him to answer my question, and then I could figure out what exactly was going on.

"Elliot Johnson. I'm Stacey's father."

Shit.

"Mr. Johnson, I don't know where your daughter is." I kept my tone even, but inside, my stomach was twisting into knots.

Any missing kid case would tear me up, I knew, but Stacey...she was Jenna's sister. And if the teenager's disappearance was related to my finding her, I'd never forgive myself.

"Like hell you don't!"

The anger was back again, but I didn't care if he was furious with me. I just needed him to believe me so that we could start looking for Stacey.

"I swear to you, Mr. Johnson, I haven't seen Stacey or talked to her. I've respected your wishes and left her alone."

"Then her sister has her. Give me the bitch's name, and I'll leave you alone."

I ignored the automatic need to protect my friend. His thirteen-year-old daughter was missing. I'd be freaking out too. Jenna would have agreed with me.

"Why?" I shook my head, trying to understand. "Does Stacey even know about her sister?"

That silenced him, but only for a moment. "Not from us, she doesn't, but I wouldn't put it past you and the woman who hired you to wreck our lives to do something behind my back."

Anger rose inside me, but I forced it down. "I certainly did no such thing, and I'll call my client to ask if she's seen or heard from Stacey, but I know this woman very well. She was disappointed that you didn't want the two of them to meet, but she understood and accepted your decision. She wouldn't have gone against your wishes, and if Stacey had come to her, she would've contacted you. At the very least, she would have called me to contact you on her behalf."

"She has to have her. It's the only explanation."

He was grasping for an answer that would allow his daughter to be safe and give him someone to be mad at, I realized. I didn't try to argue with him. Wasting time wasn't what we needed right now.

"When did you last see her?"

"This morning when she left with Roberta to hit the Black Friday sales."

Okay, that was a bit more literal than I'd meant it to be. "What about your wife? When did she last see Stacey?"

"They did their shopping and then went out to lunch. Roberta said that right before they were about to come home, Stacey excused herself to the bathroom and never came back."

I closed my eyes and prayed that someone hadn't grabbed Stacey from the restroom. On a day like today, no one would be looking at faces, trying to remember people. We'd be lucky to get a single description of anyone out of the ordinary.

"There's nothing on any of the security cameras, and

no one saw her come out of the bathroom." His voice broke. "Where's my daughter?"

"I'm going to help you find her," I promised. "I'll work things from my end and call you if I learn anything. If you need me to talk to anyone at the police department, let me know."

"They said they'd be searching for her, but..." He coughed the emotion out of his throat, and his tone hardened. "If I find out you're lying to me and her sister knows something, I'll do whatever it takes to make you pay."

I absorbed the threat and ignored it. "I'll call you if I find anything."

I ended the call and immediately went to my contacts. I hated to ruin Jenna's family time today, but she'd want to know. Besides, I needed to ask to make certain that Stacey hadn't somehow found her and called. For all I knew, Stacey had called but hadn't mentioned anything about where she was or the fact that her parents didn't know she'd left. Jenna wouldn't know that her sister was missing unless Stacey told her.

"Rona?"

"I'm sorry to do this," I said, "but I just got a call from Elliot Johnson. Stacey's missing."

Jenna gasped but quickly recovered, and in a firm voice said, "Come over."

TWENTY-TWO

"I have favors from the FBI I can call in." Jenna broke the silence that had filled the space between us almost constantly since we'd left her house a couple hours ago.

"I thought there were restrictions about when the FBI can step in." I didn't look at Jenna when I spoke. Neither of us were looking at each other, actually. Instead, we were both staring out of our respective windows, hoping that we'd see a hitch-hiking kid.

I'd barely explained my conversation with Elliot when Jenna was grabbing a jacket and rushing me out the door. It didn't matter that the Johnsons didn't want her to meet Stacey or that we really didn't have much in the way of clues about what had happened. Elliot and Roberta would be searching the obvious places – friends' houses, favorite hangouts, that sort of thing – so the two of us would look at the fringes, beginning with roads in and out of Loveland.

"Technically, you're right," she said. "But I've given the

Denver office some of their biggest arrests over the last couple years. They owe me."

Her words were as grim as her expression, and I hoped that it wouldn't come to calling in favors. If the FBI refused to help until they had cause to get involved, I didn't think Jenna would ever forgive them. In all honesty, I wasn't sure I would either.

"What are the chances she ran away?" I asked. "I know I thought about it when I was her age."

"Before your dad's accident?" Jenna shot me a look. "From what you told me, Stacey has a great home and is a good kid. She was adopted as a baby and never knew anything about it. No shit from Helen or baggage from being in some group home or bouncing from one place to another. Not even any unresolved issues from the adoption itself."

As much as I hated to admit it, Jenna was right. Stacey had been adopted, but she'd never been told. She had the same racial makeup as the Johnsons' biological daughter would have, and even looked enough like them feature-wise that she'd have no reason to question that they weren't her biological parents. And while Elliot and Roberta had been short with me, it'd been clear that they loved their daughter and didn't want anything to hurt her. They wanted to protect her. Then it struck me. Maybe that had been the problem.

"Do you think that she might think her parents are too strict?" I asked as I glanced over at my friend. "In trying to protect her, they hadn't let her do a lot?"

Jenna shrugged. "Anything's possible, I suppose."

I pulled into the parking lot to Moby Arena and parked off to the side. I turned to face Jenna. "Before we start back toward Loveland again, we need to think about where we're going. We've covered all the main routes between her parents' house and here, and driven past all the fraternity and sorority houses. If anyone's having a party, they're keeping it low-key."

"That was a long-shot anyway," Jenna said. "If a kid's going to sneak away to a party, they're not going to do it hours before it starts, and they're definitely not going to make it obvious to their parents that they're gone."

That was the part of this story that kept nagging at me. Stacey hadn't snuck out of her room or told her parents she was going to a friend's house. There'd been none of the clichéd 'rebellious teen' behavior. If she'd voluntarily left, she'd done so in a way that indicated she'd wanted her parents to know that she was gone.

Which meant the two biggest possibilities were that she'd done it with the intent to scare them...or she hadn't had a choice in the matter.

Either way, we needed to find her before things got even worse, for her *and* her parents sakes.

"If something happens to her because of me, I'll never forgive myself," Jenna said quietly. She glanced at me, then went back to staring out the windshield. "I should have just left it all alone. Let my brothers and sisters live their lives free of anyone or anything connected to our mother."

I reached over and put my hand on hers. "You're not responsible for what's happening. Stacey doesn't even know about you or Helen."

"No more," Jenna said, shaking her head. "I don't want you to look for anyone else. Once we find Stacey, we're going to walk away. I refuse to risk anyone else."

I wanted to argue with her about it, but this wasn't the time. We needed to focus on finding Stacey. Everything else could wait.

"Let's take this one step at a time," I said. "First, we find Stacey."

Jenna nodded and then sighed. "I think I know why we can't figure out where she would go."

I raised an eyebrow. "Why's that?"

"We weren't normal thirteen-year-olds."

That was an excellent point.

"We need to touch base with Elliot and Roberta," I said. "We need to know more about who Stacey is if we're going to find her."

"They won't want me there," Jenna said.

"They want to find their daughter," I countered.

"We need to be thinking outside the box," Jenna said, "not the same things as everyone else."

"What aren't we seeing then?" I asked. "We need to stop thinking emotionally. How would we come at this if it was a case?"

She might not have been a private investigator, but she had a logical way of approaching things. She thought things through, looked at issues from different angles. That's how we both needed to be looking at this problem. Not out of emotion, but from logic.

"If we were looking for a missing kid who we thought

ran away, where would we go after we eliminated friends and family?" I asked.

"It would depend on whether or not she wanted to feel safe, or if she wanted to rebel."

"Let's go for safe first," I suggested. "She'd go somewhere familiar, but if that wasn't available, she'd go with somewhere she knew but off the beaten path."

"I'm guessing her parents will have already checked the school, places of worship, that sort of thing."

"Her parents," I said suddenly.

"What?" She looked at me.

"When I was a kid, before things with my dad went... the way they went, I used to visit him at work. I loved going to the mill, seeing the crew and how they worked together. I loved the smell of the fresh cut lumber."

I swallowed around the lump in my throat. To this day, that scent brought back childhood memories, something I appreciated in private moments. Right now wasn't the time though.

"You think she went to where her parents worked?" Jenna asked. "Didn't you say that her father's a teacher?"

I nodded. "They would've already checked the school."

"What about her mother?"

I tapped the steering wheel, mentally scanning both parents' profile. "She's a real estate agent."

"Which means she might know where empty houses are," Jenna said.

"We need to talk to Roberta."

Fifteen minutes later, Jenna and I walked into Mrs.

Johnson's office. As soon as I called and told Roberta my theory, she asked me to meet her at her office.

"That's her, isn't it?" Elliot glared at us as he spoke to me. "Why the hell would you bring her here?"

"Elliot," Roberta snapped, "I don't care who she is. We need to find our daughter, and she's helping."

"How do we know she isn't the reason Stacey's missing?" Elliot asked, deep lines furrowing his forehead.

Jenna stepped forward. "I was disappointed by your decision, but I understand it. I won't go against what you want. I'll help you look for her, but I won't tell her who I am. Not unless you change your mind."

"Don't hold your breath," Elliot muttered.

Jenna ignored him and directed her question to Roberta. "Do you keep a list of the houses you're selling, the ones that are vacant?"

TWENTY-THREE

IT WAS WELL PAST MIDNIGHT BEFORE WE WENT BACK to the Johnsons' house. Jenna and I had checked every house on the list Roberta had given us, and even a couple others nearby that had looked empty. We'd kept going even after getting a text from Roberta saying that she and Elliot were going back home to see if Stacey had come back. But after another hour of nothing, we'd gone to the Johnsons' house to regroup and see if anyone had heard anything.

I had to admit, I was surprised when Roberta let us in, but Elliot didn't even blink when we walked inside. He actually looked a little shell-shocked, and I felt a wave of pity for him. No one deserved to go through something like this.

Then I thought about the woman who'd given birth to Jenna and Stacey. She would've deserved to go through this. Hell, she deserved worse than this. Elliot and Roberta, they were good parents, and I hoped I hadn't completely fucked up their lives by showing up.

I'd told Jenna that she wasn't at fault, and I'd meant it. Me, on the other hand, I should've been thinking clearly. I should've given her better advice about how to approach things.

I should have started with her older siblings, the ones who were already adults. The ones who could've made the decisions themselves and been equipped to handle the emotional impact that would come with those choices.

"What do we do now?" Roberta asked. Her dark eyes were shining with tears, and I could only imagine what it took to hold them back. She sat down next to her husband and leaned against him.

I looked at Jenna and saw my own thoughts reflected on her face. She reached into her pocket, but I shook my head. I had an FBI contact too. I'd try first, coming from the friendship angle. If that didn't work, Jenna could play the debt card with Agent Matthews. I wouldn't tell the Johnsons either way unless the FBI agreed to help. Getting their hopes up would only make things worse. Plus, I had a feeling they felt like I'd already interfered in their lives enough.

I started toward the door, intending to quietly slip out to make my call without the risk of anyone overhearing me, but I was still a few feet from the door when it opened, and Stacey walked inside.

Everything froze for several long seconds, and then everyone started talking at once.

"Where have you been?!"

"What the hell were you thinking?!"

"What's going on? Who are they?"

"We should really go."

"I think you should. Thank you for coming."

Roberta gave us both a smile as she hugged Stacey, but I knew they both wanted us gone so they could deal with whatever was going on with their daughter.

Before we could get to the door, however, Stacey raised her voice. "Wait!"

"Stacey–" I heard the warning in Elliot's voice.

"No, Dad, we need to talk, and if they're who I think they are, they need to be here too." Stacey's dark eyes moved from her parents to Jenna and me.

Roberta gestured for us to sit down, and when Elliot opened his mouth to say something, she shot him one of those looks that only wives and mothers could get away with. His mouth snapped shut, but he still glared at us.

Stacey's next words, however, caught all of our attention. "I know I'm adopted."

"What are you talking about?" Roberta's voice shook.

The girl folded her arms, a stubborn expression on her face. One that I'd seen Jenna wearing. "I've known for three years."

"How?" The question came from Elliot. "We were always so careful."

"Grandma was babysitting me, and I was doing a genealogy project for school. I dug around in your office, found the keys to the fireproof box, and I remembered you saying that it held our birth certificates, that sort of thing. I opened it up and found the paperwork for my adoption."

"I'm so sorry we never told you," Roberta said, the tears

finally spilling over. "But if you've known all this time, why did you run away tonight?"

"I didn't run away...exactly. I needed time to think."

"Think about what?" Elliot gave Jenna and me a glare.

"While Mom and I were out shopping, I overheard her side of a conversation with you."

Both Elliot and Roberta flushed, and I wondered if this was where my responsibility came in.

"I heard Mom say she wanted to know what you guys would do if my sister came around even though you'd told her not to." Stacey glanced at me, and then at Jenna, before turning back to her parents. "I hadn't really thought about whether or not I had any brothers or sisters. I hadn't really thought much about my biological family at all. But when I heard that I had a sister and she was looking for me..." Stacey shoved her hands into her pockets.

"This is something we need to talk about," Elliot said. "You, your mother, and I. *After* we discuss what you did."

Stacey shook her head. "I'm sorry for making you worry, but I needed to think about how you two have been lying to me my whole life. Adopted. A sister. You two always went on and on about honesty, and you've been hiding all this from me?"

Roberta reached out and took her daughter's hand. "I'm so sorry. We were scared that you might want to find them, that you'd want to leave us and be with them." She looked at Jenna, then at me, a glint of determination in her eyes. "This young lady," she gestured to me, "is Rona Quick. She's a private investigator that came to your father and me on behalf of your sister."

I gave Stacey an uncomfortable smile and a little wave.

"Roberta," Elliot hissed, glowering at his wife.

"I'm doing this, Elliot," Roberta said firmly. "I won't lose our daughter because we're too scared to tell her the truth."

"You're my parents," Stacey said, her voice softening. "You've raised me, and you love me. You won't lose me just because I have a bigger family."

She wrapped her arms around Roberta, and a moment later, Elliot got up and joined the embrace. Feeling like I was intruding, I looked over at Jenna, who only shrugged. We might be able to slip away now, but if we did, Jenna might miss actually being introduced to her sister. As Roberta stepped back, she wiped her eyes and smiled at Jenna.

"Stacey, this is your sister, Jenna Archer. She's been wanting to meet you for a while."

Jenna stood up, and I saw her hands shake as she rubbed her palms on her jeans. I couldn't hold back the smile as she moved forward to greet the first of her siblings. Hopefully, the other introductions would be a lot less eventful.

TWENTY-FOUR

When I'd been figuring out what I wanted to do this weekend, it hadn't included driving all over the city for hours on end, looking for a missing thirteen-year-old, and I certainly hadn't thought I'd be involved in a strange sort of family reunion.

Jenna was quiet as I drove her home. A different kind of quiet than she usually was. My own thoughts kept running over and over everything that had happened in the past twenty-four hours, and I knew that Jenna was thinking about it too.

This had been the first of her siblings that she'd met, and one who'd never lived with their mother, not even for a few months. Stacey was the same age Jenna had been when she'd been rescued from her mother, and I couldn't help wondering if Jenna saw that in her sister. The life Jenna could have had if she'd been born to a decent person. All of that potential. All of the love and support that would have nurtured her natural talents.

Would this make her reconsider having me look for the rest of her brothers and sisters? I hoped not.

I wasn't worried about the billable hours I'd lose if she asked me to stop. I agreed with her reasons for wanting to find the others in the first place, but I couldn't say that I understood what she was going through. What I, as an outsider, might think was important might be the last thing Jenna cared about. Whatever my friend decided, I would support her.

As I pulled into her driveway, I finally spoke, "I'm here if you want to talk about any of this."

She gave me a tight smile and nodded. "Thanks. I think I'm going to wait to make any decisions until I've showered, slept, and eaten. I need a clear head."

"Any time you want to talk, just call."

She thanked me again as Rylan opened her door. The moment she was on her feet, he had his arms around her. She buried her face against his chest, and I looked away, not wanting to intrude on such a personal moment.

I turned on the radio as I made my way back down the driveway, needing something to keep my brain from taking off down some rabbit hole. I had too much to think about, and she was right. Shower, bed, food. After that, I could focus on the things bouncing around in my head.

My stomach growled, but I was too tired to even consider stopping somewhere. I was barely safe driving as it was. If I lost momentum, I'd probably fall asleep at the wheel. At the rate I was going, there was a possibility I'd even fall asleep in the shower, but that one was a risk I was willing to take.

I pulled into my parking space and gave a sigh of relief. Stairs, bathroom, shower, bedroom, bed. Maybe a stop in the kitchen. I'd see where my feet took me. First, I had stairs to contend with. Stairs and snow, I saw as I got out of the car. When had that started?

For the first time since Adare died, I thought that it might not be too bad to move into the apartment above the office. I was renting my place by the month without a contract, but I wanted to give at least a month's notice. If I did it now, I could be in the other apartment by the first of the year and avoid having to use outside steps through the rest of winter. Some days, I wouldn't even need to go outside at all.

The idea was appealing, but I wasn't in any shape to give serious consideration to it. Stairs first.

I was almost to the top when I realized that someone was standing at my door. Judging by the way Jalen was glaring at me, he'd been out in the cold and wet for a while. I tried to muster up some sympathy, but I was too exhausted to feel much of anything.

"Morning," I said as I stepped past him to unlock the door. I held it open as I walked inside, figuring he'd follow. Whatever he'd come here for, he could say it while I grabbed a semi-stale muffin.

"*Morning?* That's all I get?"

He was in a pleasant mood.

"You stand me up last night, ignore my calls and texts so I'm freaking out that something's happened to you. I call Rylan and have to hear from *him* that you're out with Jenna. I'm glad the two of you are friends, but I think I should've at least gotten a text to let me know you weren't coming."

Shit.

We had plans last night, and I'd completely forgotten about them. I'd even kept my phone on during my conversation with Roberta so I wouldn't miss any texts from her, and I hadn't bothered to check out any other notifications.

"I'm sorry," I said, throwing away the muffin wrapper. "I got caught up in what was going on and completely forgot."

"What was so important that you'd blow me off and not have the decency to answer me?"

I frowned. This was my fault. I freely admitted that. But he was out of line coming at me like that after I'd apologized. I didn't plan on giving him details because Jenna was a client and I did my best to keep client's information private, even if I was talking to someone who knew them, but his attitude made it easier to be blunt about it.

"Where I was and what I was doing is between Jenna and myself." I took a bottle of water from my fridge and drank half of it. I was still hungry, but I'd taken the edge off enough that I'd be able to sleep.

"That's the way things are going to go between us then," he said with a bark of a laugh. "I have to tell you everything, and you get to keep whatever you want from me. Go out to lunch with your ex, hang out with your friend. Expect me to sit around waiting until you decide to show up."

I was not in the mood for this, but I figured I'd at least try.

"I apologized," I countered. "Both for not telling you about my lunch with Clay, and for not calling you last night."

"Only after I called you out on both of them." He crossed his arms, a muscle in his jaw clenching.

Nope. I wasn't going to do this. Not here. Not now. I'd admitted that I was wrong and apologized. Both times. If he couldn't accept that, or even see that I wasn't even close to being capable of having this conversation at the moment, then I was through being polite. I didn't have the patience for it.

"Look, I'm exhausted," I said, meeting his angry gaze and giving a level one in return. "I apologized. If you can't accept that, it's your problem, not mine."

His mouth flattened into a thin line. "I think I deserve an explanation."

I had a whole other idea about what he deserved, but I wasn't taking the bait. "I'm not doing this. You need to go."

His jaw dropped, and a flush flooded his face. "You can't just kick me out before we talked things through."

I'd had more than enough. "Fine. Stay. I don't give a damn. I need a shower and bed. If you want to sit out here and sulk like a child, you're welcome to do it as long as you do it quietly. Otherwise, get the hell out of my apartment, and we'll finish this some other time."

I didn't wait to hear him argue or see if he stayed or went. I walked straight into the bathroom, closed the door, and turned on the shower. Whatever he decided, that was on him. Unless he tried to keep talking to me when I'd told him to be quiet or leave. If that happened, he and I were going to have an even bigger problem than we had already.

I showered quickly, and by the time I was done, the apartment was empty. I didn't even bother dressing before falling into bed and wrapping myself up in my sheets and blanket. The insanity of the world would be here when I woke up in a few hours.

Sleep claimed me even as my head met my pillow.

TWENTY-FIVE

One positive thing I could say for Jalen and me bickering, I wasn't even tempted to put off any work I had to do. I'd slept through most of Saturday, then started working like crazy first thing Sunday morning, some on finding Jenna's other siblings, some on a few other possible cases I'd come up with on my own.

Missing kids. Fort Collins, Loveland, the whole area. To start, anyway. The cops would have some of these cases, the ones where the parents had filed reports, but others would be the sorts of kids who didn't have adults looking out for them, the kids who were on the streets here to escape from something worse elsewhere.

Some of the disappeared would be runaways. Some would be dead.

Some would have been taken like Meka, but without anyone looking for them, they would vanish.

I was going to do whatever it took to make sure that didn't happen. When Jenna gave me leads to follow, I'd do it, but I didn't plan on limiting my work to the specific assignments I was given. I had a feeling some of the people in my life would have something to say about that, but I didn't care. I'd found something I could fight for.

All of that was why I was back at the county courthouse, hoping I wouldn't be condemned to that same musty basement room where I'd spent too many hours already.

"Next." A far too happy, sandy-haired man beamed at me. "How can I help you?"

"I need to see census records. Hard copies."

He blinked. "From where and when?"

"Whatever ones you have here."

His smile faltered, and he shifted in his seat. "Miss, we have copies of records from five counties, going back twenty years."

I smiled and hoped he didn't think I was laughing at how pale his face had gotten. "Then that's what I want."

As I followed the directions he'd given me, I thought back to the call I'd gotten from Jenna a few hours ago. Technically, what I was doing was checking out an idea that she'd had rather than something specific Agent Matthews had asked of her. The fact that it would help me with what I was doing was just icing on the cake.

Jenna had no problem accessing digital census records, but a few things she'd found made her wonder if those records were as accurate as they should have been. She hadn't given me a reason why she suspected that, but I hadn't needed her to. If she asked me to go look at the hard copies, then that was what I would do. I'd look for evidence of tampering on the hard copies and take pictures I'd later send to Jenna. It would take a long time to compare the digital copies to the hard copies, so I wouldn't do that here and now. If Jenna wanted me to help with the comparison, she'd ask.

I planned on keeping the census pictures for my project too. I could compare one year to the next and find the missing names, the kids no one reported missing. It wouldn't help me with the street kids, but it was more information than I could find with just filed reports.

The room with the papers I wanted was much nicer than the previous one. This one had windows.

I started with the previous year's findings and took a deep breath before wading in. This was going to be tedious, intensive work that I wouldn't be able to finish today. Hours of poring over papers, with nothing but the same to look forward to for the rest of the week, at least. Normally, that would drive me crazy, but this sort of detail-oriented work was what I needed to keep myself from remembering that it'd been three days since Jalen had shown up at my place, and three days since I'd last heard from him.

But that wasn't important. I had details to focus on.

———

WHEN I SAW the figure standing in front of my apartment door, my heart leaped. Then I realized that this figure, while still tall, was a few inches shy of Jalen's height. The shoulders weren't quite as broad.

Still, it was a figure I knew and cared about.

"Clay, I wasn't expecting to see you."

He grinned at me as he pushed off the railing. He rubbed his hands together, then blew on them. "Thanks for showing up before things started freezing off."

I unlocked the door. "Come in. I wouldn't want to be responsible for things freezing off."

He laughed, and it brought my first real smile in days. I'd forgotten how good it felt to be with someone who made me laugh rather than someone who infuriated me. I still wanted Jalen, despite our argument, and I believed that he'd come to his senses soon. When that time came, we'd talk things out, but it was nice not to need to think at the moment.

I kicked off my shoes and Clay did the same. "Do you want something to eat? I'm starving."

"Long day?" he asked as he followed me into the kitchen. "Does county-wide courthouse research always build up an appetite?"

I threw a sharp look over my shoulder as I rummaged in my freezer for my last frozen pizza. "Do I even want to know how you know that?"

"Probably not," he admitted as he reached over to pre-heat the oven.

"But you're going to tell me anyway," I said. I opened the box and scowled. This thing was going to taste like cardboard.

"When someone comes along asking for something like every available census record for the past twenty years, it tends to get noticed."

I slid the pizza into the oven and tried to decide if I was creeped out, annoyed, or indifferent to the fact that the FBI knew what I'd been doing today. "Did that overly-enthusiastic guy at the courthouse call you or something? Do you have them looking for me?"

I was going with annoyed, apparently.

Clay rolled his eyes. "Way too high for my pay grade. I can barely order coffee on my own. Besides the fact that I'd never do something like that to you, I don't have even close to that sort of authority."

I raised an eyebrow and folded my arms. "What about your partner? Does Agent Matthews have that sort of authority? Does he have Jenna and me doing his dirty work while he spies on us?"

Clay's expression sobered. "He wouldn't do anything to hurt Jenna. Ray's on the up-and-up. He looks at her like a little sister."

"Then how did you know exactly what I was doing and where I was doing it?"

He sighed. "That's an excellent question." He walked over to the fridge and took out a beer. "Here's what I know. I was sitting at my desk, finishing some paperwork when Special Agent Diaz came to my desk and told me that I needed to pay you a visit. He said he got a call that you were 'ruffling some feathers' and you needed to leave things alone."

Someone in authority higher than a special agent in the FBI had eyes on Jenna and me.

I really hoped it didn't mean what I thought it meant.

TWENTY-SIX

"Rona! Wake up! Rona!"

I groaned and rolled over. Who was pounding on my bedroom door? My sleep-addled brain couldn't place the voice even though whoever he was, he knew my name.

Suddenly, my hands came in contact with a very firm, and very hot, surface. A surface that felt an awful lot like a muscular chest. A bare one.

And then something just as hot and firm brushed against my thigh, and I realized I was naked too.

My eyes flew open as a pair of strong arms wrapped around me, and I found myself staring into a pair of beautiful and familiar eyes. He smiled, and those eyes sparkled, little crinkles appearing at the corners.

"Hey, gorgeous."

His sleep-roughened voice sent a wave of heat washing over my skin and pooling between my legs.

"Rona!" Another series of knocks, just as impatient as the voice sounded.

"Are you going to tell your brother you're awake, or do you want me to?"

My heart gave an unsteady thump. "My brother?"

The wrongness of the situation hit me all at once. Where was I? Why was he *in my bed? And why did he think I had a brother?*

"I could tell Freddie that we decided it would be a good idea for me to sneak out of the guest room because you thought it'd be hot to have sex in your childhood bedroom, but I'd really like for your dad not to kill me."

I gave him a sharp look, but the only humor on his face was good-natured. He was really joking about my father killing him.

What the hell *was going on here?*

I looked around. Yes, this did look like my old bedroom, but it also looked a little more...mature. More like the room of a teenager heading off to college rather than a girl on the brink of adolescence.

Even as I took in the details, the full impact of what he said hit me. "Wait, are you saying my dad's here?" A bright flare of panic shot through me as I sat up, barely catching the sheet against my breasts.

"Of course he's here." He sat up too, a puzzled expression on his face. "Rona, are you okay?"

I shook my head. "I don't understand. I shouldn't be here. This isn't right. I live in Colorado. I don't have any family. You shouldn't be here. I'm with Jalen. Where's Jalen?"

Clay's expression was concerned as he put his hand on my shoulder, but he tried to make his tone light. "Should I be worried that you're asking about another man hours before our wedding?"

"Our what?" The words came out as a whisper instead of the shout I'd intended.

Clay opened his mouth, but no sound came out. He looked like he thought he was talking but all I heard was muffled voices growing louder. Yelling. Pulling me toward them. Faster and faster until...

"You need to answer my question about what the *fuck* you're doing here!"

"That's none of your damn business." Clay's voice was lower, but still loud enough for me to hear what he was saying. "You need to leave before you wake her up."

The bitter laugh that came next was enough to get me out of bed. I stepped into the living room just as Jalen started talking again.

"Weren't you able to wear her out enough last night that she'll sleep right through this?"

"What's going on here?" I didn't raise my voice, but both men turned toward me.

Clay wore a pair of jeans I assumed he'd gotten from the emergency travel pack he kept in his car, but he hadn't put on a shirt or shoes. With a towel over his shoulder and a spatula in hand, he definitely looked comfortable in my apartment.

Jalen looked rumpled, as if he hadn't slept well in a while. He was carrying a box of donuts and a bouquet of assorted flowers, both of which suggested he'd come here to talk about our argument the other night.

"I don't think I'm the one who needs to offer an explanation," Jalen said. "I wanted to apologize for getting upset the other night, but instead of you answering the door, *he* does, dressed like that and telling me that you're 'still in bed.'"

I crossed my arms and tried not to feel self-conscious about the fact that I wasn't wearing a bra under the thin t-shirt I'd worn to bed last night. I was glad it was cool enough in here that I'd worn sweats rather than just underwear. Otherwise this would've been a lot worse.

"What is it you want to apologize about?" I asked.

Jalen's fingers tightened around the base of the flowers. "I wanted to apologize because Jenna told me what happened the night you stood me up. That she was the client you were working for and that you were helping her find her sister who'd taken off."

A flash of anger went through me, and I pushed it down as I asked, "Is that the only reason?"

He scowled at me. "What other reason do you want?"

My temper bubbled up again, and I wondered how I'd been able to keep it this long. "I don't know. It might've been nice if you'd simply accepted my apology and waited until I wasn't exhausted to talk instead of skulking off and ignoring me for days."

"You could've called me," he pointed out. "You know, instead of running to Clay like you always do."

"You need to back off," Clay said, somehow managing to look threatening while pointing a spatula at Jalen.

"Let me handle this," I said to him. I took a step toward Jalen. "Okay, we both could've picked up the phone, but that doesn't give you an excuse to come barging into my apartment, yelling and making accusations."

"Accusations? Really?" Jalen sneered. "This is the second time I've shown up at your apartment early in the morning and found him half-dressed and you looking freshly fucked."

Heat flooded my face, as much from anger as from embarrassment. "How *dare* you come in here and say that to me!"

"Oh, was it *making love* then?" He threw the box of donuts at the closest table. "Guess that makes me the pity fuck, right? You two get together and laugh about it? About how stupid I am for believing you the last time I caught you two like this, and you said nothing happened?"

"Yeah, Jalen, it's the whole world ganging up against you." I shook my head as my voice dropped. I was still pissed, but that wasn't the dominant emotion anymore. "You decide how the world is and that makes it so. Must be nice to know everything."

"I actually thought you were different." He dropped the flowers, stepping on them as he left.

"Bastard!" I shouted as he slammed the door shut behind him.

Tears burned against my eyelids, but I pushed them back. No way in *hell* was I going to cry over Jalen Larsen. Not anymore. I was done with him and his inability to trust. I'd thought I had issues, but I was nothing compared to him.

"Rona, are you okay?" Clay put his hand on my shoulder.

"Fine." I glanced at him. "But would it kill you to wear a damn shirt?"

"We both know it's not about me not wearing a shirt."

He had a point.

"I'm sorry for my part in it," he said. "I shouldn't have let him come in. I thought you knew he was coming."

"It's not your fault," I said, moving out from under Clay's well-meaning hand. Between my dream and Jalen's accusations, I wasn't feeling particularly comfortable with my friend touching me right now.

"Did you tell Jalen that you and I used to...be a thing?"

"I did," I said as I picked up the flowers and set them on the counter. Some of them were crushed, but I was still going to check to see if any of them could be salvaged. No point in wasting them. "And I also told him that it was over. That we're friends."

"You have to admit," Clay said, "from his side of things, it did look pretty bad."

I almost threw the donuts at him, but it would've been a waste of good sugar. "What's that supposed to mean?"

"I'm just saying, I know I'd be pissed if I showed up at my girlfriend's place some morning and a gorgeous, shirtless man answered the door."

"Gorgeous?" I raised an eyebrow. "You think a little highly of yourself."

He grinned at me, but I didn't quite have it in me to smile back.

"Anyway, it doesn't matter," I said. "I don't care what it looked like. He's crossed the line more than once."

"Don't you think it's because he's scared?" He held up

a hand when I opened my mouth to argue. "He is, Rona. He's absolutely terrified that he's going to lose you."

"Then he should talk to me instead of behaving like a child," I countered. "He should trust me."

A little voice in the back of my head reminded me that Jalen had good reason to be untrusting. Elise had done a number on him.

But he should know that I wasn't Elise. It wasn't fair to me to be held responsible for the infidelities of his crazy ex-wife...excuse me, *wife*. Besides, it wasn't like I didn't have my own baggage from my past to deal with. He'd seen most of it.

Maybe that was the problem. He needed someone who could handle his shit without him having to deal with theirs. The thing was, I had no problem working with him on his issues. It seemed like he didn't want to try to get better though. He just wanted me to accept things the way they were. Maybe some women could do that, but I couldn't.

TWENTY-SEVEN

I PROBABLY SHOULDN'T HAVE EATEN THAT SECOND donut, but it'd been either a chocolate donut with sprinkles or a shot of tequila, and I didn't think alcohol before work was the best idea. So, I'd gone with sugar, and now I was having a serious sugar crash.

I stared at the computer screen, reading the same email for the third or fourth time, but not processing it any better than I had the first time. It wasn't even an email that I would've read thoroughly before. A privacy policy change that I normally would've skimmed. Except today, I couldn't seem to get past it. I'd move on to the next one, but then I'd start getting anxious, worried that I'd miss something important, and that would send me back to the email. It wasn't rational, but the brain wasn't always rational.

I needed to pull myself together. I'd done it before, multiple times, and under much more difficult circumstances. After what happened with my parents, I'd made a new life with Anton. After he died, I made another new life, this one alone. When I'd lost my place at the academy, I hadn't known what I'd do. Then I'd come here and decided that this was where I wanted to start again. *Again*.

Except I didn't want to uproot my life again. This was my new life, and I wasn't going to let what happened with Jalen scare me away from a city I loved, a job that made a difference, and friends like Jenna, Rylan, and Clay.

Which meant I needed to get through this damned email before my one o'clock appointment with a potential receptionist.

Still, I breathed a sigh of relief when I heard someone come in. A client was an excuse that my brain understood.

"Hey, are you busy?" Jenna came back into the office with a smile. "If you are, that's fine, but if not, I'd like to talk about my cases."

"Anything specific you want to talk about?" I asked, speaking way too fast. "Help yourself to coffee and donuts too. I've had way too many of both."

"I talked to Stacey again yesterday," she said as she poured herself something to drink. "Her parents grounded her for a month for taking off instead of talking to them, but I have a feeling they're going to cave and let her out early. They're having some serious guilt about hiding the truth from her."

"I couldn't imagine what I'd do in their position," I admitted. "Deciding whether or not to tell a kid they were adopted. When to do it. How."

"She's actually more frustrated with them for keeping me from her than she is about the adoption thing." Jenna sat across from me and reached into the box to pull out one of the jelly-filled donuts. "But they've made it very clear that I'm not supposed to tell Stacey any of the...bad. I completely get it. They want to protect her. But it does make it harder for me to be honest about my past, which makes it harder for her to get to know me."

"What do you tell her?" I asked.

"What I can," Jenna said and licked some sugar from her finger. "If it's something her parents don't want me to talk about, I keep it vague and say that maybe I'll tell her more when she's older. I'm pretty sure she tried googling me, so she knows there's some bad stuff in my past."

Bad stuff. That was an understatement.

"Does that mean you've changed your mind about not wanting to find the rest of your siblings?" I'd wondered how resolved she would continue to be about that or if it'd been more of a heat of the moment sort of decision.

"I'm not sure," she admitted. "Searching for Stacey did put her into danger."

"Danger of her own making," I put in. "Hers and her parents. If they'd been honest with her, she might not have reacted the way she did."

"True, but we can't know what any of my other siblings know about who they are or where they come from. Or how they'll react when we find them." She took a thoughtful bite of her donut.

"I can gather the information and then let you decide if you want to reach out," I said. "Just because I find them doesn't mean they need to know."

Jenna sighed, her expression sober. "What do you

think, Rona? Do you think I'm being selfish, wanting to find them, wanting them to be in my life?"

I leaned toward her, resting my elbows on the desk. "You're far from selfish, Jenna. If I was in your position, if I had a chance to have family that wasn't my psychotic father, I'd take it."

She finished the last of her coffee and got up to pour herself another cup. When she sat back down, she looked at me. "Okay. Keep looking, but don't approach them or their families. I'll decide if I want to do that once you have another name or two for me."

I nodded and finished my own coffee. I didn't get up for more. I had way too much caffeine in my system as it was. "I'm glad you came by. I needed to talk to you about those census records you had me get."

"I've got an algorithm running on the files I have and the pictures you sent me. I should know more about any discrepancies soon."

"That's great, but it's not about that." I thought for a moment, then amended, "Well, it sort of is. When I got home from the courthouse yesterday, Clay was waiting for me." I ignored the stab of pain that came with the memory of the things that followed. "He told me that I was ruffling feathers."

Jenna straightened, her eyes narrowing. "What?"

I recounted my conversation with Clay as close to word-for-word as I could manage it but didn't add in any of my personal thoughts on the matter. As I spoke, I watched Jenna's eyes darken and her mouth twist into a scowl. When I finished, I leaned back and waited for her reaction.

"Fuck me," she breathed, shaking her head. "Someone's up to no good."

"So, it's not just me then?" I asked, leaning back in my chair. "I'm not the only one who thinks it's suspicious?"

She tapped her index finger to her lip, looking thoughtfully at the wall. "I can't believe how blatant that was. Maybe that's why they thought no one would think anything of it. Because only an *idiot* would run things down the chain of command like that."

"Unless whoever needs us to stop digging into things chose messengers who wouldn't be traced back to them. You said Clay only knew who told him to talk to you, and you're certain that he's not into anything shady?"

I didn't even have to think about it. "He's not. Especially not in anything like human trafficking."

"Which is probably why he was the perfect choice to talk to you. He probably thinks it's because of some investigation that's being worked already."

I nodded. "I didn't ask him, but that sounds like what he'd think."

"I trust Agent Matthews," Jenna said, "and you trust Clay, but I think you and I need to make sure we play things close to the vest. We need to be careful of what we tell even them. We don't want to put them into a position where they'll get caught in the middle."

I loved that she hadn't even suggested that the smartest thing to do would be to drop the investigation and move elsewhere. Neither one of us were going to walk away from this. If anything, we were both more determined than ever to root out every bit of corruption and filth we could reach.

Those assholes wouldn't know what hit them.

TWENTY-EIGHT

On paper, Maggie Carlyle was a risk. Twenty-eight years old, and she'd had more than a dozen jobs in a decade. Not just different jobs, but different addresses all over the country. She'd worked at a toy store in Boise, Idaho, and a shoe store in Miami, Florida. She'd been a housekeeper in Sacramento, and a seamstress in Austin. Her job ranged from the banal to the unique.

Still, something in my gut told me to bring her in, and after talking to her for the past ten minutes, I was glad I had. She was energetic and sweet, willing to work hard. Her references were glowing, despite the fact that she'd never worked any place longer than seven or eight months.

"One final question," I said as I put down my pen. "And I'm sure you already know what I'm going to ask."

Her smile faltered a bit, and the light in her eyes dimmed, but she squared her shoulders and nodded. "I do, and I understand why you need to know. I've moved around a lot, had tons of different jobs. I know how it looks, like I'm not reliable. I won't lie and say that I plan to be here for years, but I can promise that I will show up on time, and I won't leave early. I rarely call off, and I always work hard."

She paused, and I knew she was waiting for me to tell her none of that mattered. Instead, I made a gesture for her to continue.

"I didn't have a stable childhood, but I've always wanted to find a home." Her fair complexion flooded with color, but she didn't flinch. "After I graduated high school, I didn't really have anywhere to live, so I got on a bus and left. I tried different places, but nothing ever...stuck."

I wanted to reach across the desk and tell her that I understood, but I wasn't looking for a friend. I needed an employee first. I didn't think she'd take advantage of me if I was more friendly than professional, but as I'd proven recently, I wasn't the best judge of character when it came to people I hadn't known long.

"I've never left an employer in the lurch," she continued. "If I'm going to leave, I'll tell you and give you as much time as you need to find someone to take my place."

I had the strangest sense of déjà vu as I looked at her, but it wasn't because I'd been in this position before. I'd been *her* only a few months ago. A stranger in the city, looking for a job after having moved around because nowhere felt like home.

"I'd like to see if this would work for us," I said with a smile. "Can you start first thing Monday morning?"

Her entire face lit up. "I can. Thank you, Miss Quick. Thank you."

"You can call me Rona," I said.

Before I could move anywhere past that, the front door opened. Shit. I'd forgotten to turn over the sign to say that we were *closed*. It was a Wednesday afternoon, and the weather was shitty, so I hadn't expected anyone to come by.

"Hello?"

"I'll be right out," I called before turning back to Maggie. "Monday, eight o'clock."

She stood and shook my hand. "I'll see you then."

I followed her out of the office, turning my attention to the tall, burly man brushing snow off his massive beard. "I'm Rona Quick." I put out my hand. "How can I help you?"

"I'm Dave Orville." His hand engulfed mine, but he was careful not to squeeze too hard. "My Suzie's missing."

"I'm sorry to hear that," I said. I motioned to my office.

"I don't need much of your time, miss," he said, shifting from one foot to the other. "I just need to know if I can hire you to find my Suzie."

"I'm often hired to find people." If he didn't want to sit, that was fine with me. "Do you have a picture of Suzie?"

The best thing about smartphones was that most people had at least one picture on it of whoever it was they wanted me to find. Sure enough, he held out his phone with a picture pulled up on it.

Suzie was a cocker spaniel.

I bit back the sigh that wanted to escape me and smiled up at him. "When did you last see Suzie?"

I SHIVERED and pulled my coat more closely around me. I was crazy for taking this case, but Dave had been sincerely upset that he hadn't been able to find his little dog after she slipped off her leash during their morning walk, and there was something about seeing a man like him so distraught over his dog that had made me want to help him.

Besides, if I hadn't taken his case, I would've gone back to staring at that stupid email I couldn't get through while trying not to think about Jalen.

"Suzie," I called as I walked down the street.

I doubted that calling the dog would do much good since she didn't know me, but I felt pretty foolish walking with a dog leash in one hand and a treat in the other. Calling for a dog at least made it clear I was searching. If someone had found her and they heard me calling, they'd know to bring her to me.

I'd sent Dave back to his house in case the dog found her way home. That's what I was hoping for, anyway. I didn't know much about the intelligence of different dog breeds, but I thought spaniels might be smart ones. And there were always stories about how dogs found their way home.

I turned onto the next street, and a prickle went down my spine. I stopped, nearly slipping on the sidewalk. Someone was watching me. Again. I could feel it, a gaze burning into my back. I looked around and snowflakes caught on my lashes. I blinked them away, my vision blurring for a few seconds. When it cleared, I saw a few people on the other side of the street, a few ahead of me, and some behind. Not crowded at all, but not too sparse either.

I didn't see anyone paying any extra attention to me, or any attention, actually. It must've just been one of those weird things. Like a chill when it wasn't cold or the sense of another presence when alone.

I turned back around and resumed walking, calling for Suzie. I passed a couple of elderly women who smiled at me, and I smiled back. They probably thought I was looking for my own dog, but the only dog I'd ever had died years ago. He'd been one of those big mutts that looked scary but was really a big softie. My parents had gotten him before I was born, and he'd been my protector from moment one.

He died when I was ten, and I sometimes wondered if things would've gone differently that day if he'd still been around. Would he have been able to stop my dad from attacking my mom? Or if he would've been with me, my mom might have still died, but Petey might've been able to stop my dad before he hurt me, before he killed the others.

It wasn't the first time I'd thought of that. Nearly a decade was a long time to come up with plenty of 'what-if' scenarios. What if we'd gotten another dog? What if Petey had still been alive? What if I'd spent the night at a friend's house? What if Mom and I had left Dad when he started acting weird? What if Dad hadn't gone to work that day? What if he'd followed all the safety precautions he was supposed to?

I'd quickly learned that it was easy to get buried in

those 'what-if's, buried so deep that I lost sight of what I did have. Anton had helped me through it the first time, and I'd dealt with it myself after he died. The desire to head down that path was still there, and sometimes it was hard to stop myself, but today, I was able to move past it because I had something more important to focus on.

Namely, a cocker spaniel named Suzie.

I'd gone another three blocks when my phone rang. I pulled it out of my pocket and saw that it was Dave.

"Hello?"

"She came home!" In the background, I could hear a dog barking, and I smiled. "I was walking around my yard, calling for her and telling her that I wasn't going to be mad if she just came home. Then there she was, running toward me. Thank you so much for helping me!"

"I'm glad to hear she's home," I said, genuinely happy and relieved for them both, "but I didn't really do anything."

"Yes, you did," he insisted. "I wouldn't have gone home if you hadn't taken my case, and she would've come back and seen I wasn't there. She would've run away again."

I wasn't sure that's how things would've gone, but if he wanted to thank me, that was fine. I'd only been out here a couple hours, so I wouldn't even bother sending him a bill. I was sure he was the sort of guy who'd talk about what'd happened, and good press was worth a few hours of cold.

"I'm glad she's home," I repeated. "Go take care of her and have a nice rest of your day."

He said goodbye, and I put my phone back in my pocket. Good. I was done. I could head back to my car and go home. I had some leftovers and a nice warm couch calling my name.

I started to turn when it happened again. The feel of someone watching me.

And then pain, sharp and explosive across the back of my skull. Pain in my knees as I dropped to the ground.

Then...nothing.

TWENTY-NINE

Ouch.

My knees hurt. My head hurt. My shoulder and the palms of my hands hurt.

I'd only blacked out for a few seconds, and I honestly wasn't sure if I'd passed out or just closed my eyes and was disoriented.

I remembered landing on my knees, and then I was on the sidewalk, without anything in between. Someone pulled on my purse – hard – jerking my left shoulder painfully. My left palm scraped against concrete and ice, leaving a road-rash like scrape that felt like it matched the one already burning my right palm. My wrist ached too, and I wondered if I'd sprained it when I landed. It didn't hurt bad enough for it to be broken, or at least that's what I was hoping.

Time slipped again, and I was vaguely aware that someone was talking to me, helping me to my feet. I heard my voice telling them that I was okay, that I didn't need an ambulance, but the words seemed to come from far away. Then I looked down at the woman who was holding onto my arm, and she reminded me so much of my mother that I burst into tears.

She put her arms around me, and the gesture completely undid me. I clung to her for what seemed like hours, and she never told me that she had to go or that I shouldn't be crying. Instead, she told me that it was going to be okay and offered me a tissue. When I finally released her and took a step back, embarrassment hit me, but she simply smiled and squeezed my hand.

"You need to go to the hospital," she said, her dark eyes warm.

I shook my head. "It's nothing."

"You're bleeding, and you should get some x-rays and probably a CT scan." The stern look she gave me made me think she either had kids or was a teacher, possibly both. "You don't want to take risks with your health."

The concern in her voice almost set me off again. "I'm not parked that far away," I began, then stopped when I realized that my purse was gone.

I'd just been mugged.

I wasn't sure why it surprised me, but it did.

"I don't have my keys."

"I live right here," the stranger said. "Let me drive you, and then we can see about calling someone for you."

I followed her but didn't tell her that I didn't have anyone to call. No family. No parents or siblings or spouse. I doubted I even had a boyfriend anymore. Clay was a possibility, I supposed, but I didn't want to ask him to drive in from Denver because I didn't have car keys. Okay, it wasn't as if I'd lost my keys or something simple like that, but I couldn't keep calling Clay about my problems. He was my friend, but if I kept going to him about things like this, I was afraid the line would get blurred, and I'd end up losing him too.

"My name's Patty McBride," she said as she got behind the wheel of a surprisingly flashy sports car.

"Rona Quick," I said, running my fingers over the lock and window buttons in an attempt to distract myself from the way my palms were stinging. "I'm getting blood on your car."

She laughed, and I turned to look at her. The look she gave me was pure mischief. "It's not my car."

I stared at her, not entirely sure what she meant by that.

"This thing is my soon-to-be-ex-husband's baby. I used to say that he cared more about it than he did about me, and he never argued the point." She turned down the street where my car was, but I didn't mention it, too curious now to interrupt her. "Three days ago, he took the tickets for our Caribbean cruise and left me a note saying that his twenty-year-old yoga instructor looked better in a bikini than I did."

"Bastard."

"And then some," she said with a tight smile. "He's always underestimated me. The minute I found his note, I vowed that he'd done it a last time. While he's on that ship, I'm taking care of business here. I called up an old friend from high school who's a divorce attorney, and we're going to make sure Carl's left with nothing but those tickets and his new girlfriend."

I wasn't sure if she'd decided to tell me all that so I didn't feel bad about bleeding on the upholstery, or if she needed to tell someone who didn't have a previous stake in the relationship. Either way, her story distracted me enough that I was able to regain my composure by the time we arrived at the hospital.

Despite my protests that I could manage from there, she followed me inside and sat with me until I was called back to see a doctor. As I told her goodbye, I knew I'd never be able to fully explain to her how much it meant to have had her caring for me the way she did, but I promised myself that I'd contact her soon with an offer of my services free of charge. I'd make sure that her lawyer had all the ammunition needed to take her lousy ex to the cleaners.

With that cheery thought in my mind, I followed the nurse back to a curtained-off area where I'd be taken care of.

"WHEN DID you first notice someone following you?" The detective taking my statement barely looked old enough to shave, but it was the nervous way he kept looking at his older, grizzled partner that made me think this was his first case, or at least the first one he was taking lead on.

"I didn't." My tone was patient, even if nothing else

about me was. I understood that someone had to be the kid's first, and I was trying to remember that as he fumbled his way through questions, but I really wanted to go home and take a nice, hot bath, then crawl into my bed. Then again, I supposed it was better to have him starting out on a mugging rather than a sexual assault or a murder or something like that.

"I thought you said..." He flipped back through his notes.

"I said that I felt like someone was watching me," I corrected. "But when I looked, I couldn't see anyone specific. There were other people on the sidewalk, but no one looked suspicious."

"Would you be willing to work with a sketch artist?" The kid's Adam's apple bobbed as he swallowed hard. "I mean, if you think that would help you remember."

I gave him a tight smile. "I was hit from behind, then fell forward. I didn't see anyone until Patty helped me up. A sketch artist won't be able to do any good with that."

"Miss Quick, can you think of anyone who might want to hurt you?" The other detective broke in, giving his partner a sharp look. "As a private investigator, I'm sure you've had your fair share of unhappy clients."

Evan Lee's face flashed into my mind. "A couple," I admitted, "but no one's threatened me. They've called me incompetent, that sort of thing, but no one said they were going to hurt me."

"No unhappy ex-boyfriends?" the kid asked. His cheeks suddenly flushed. "Or ex-girlfriends?"

"No." Jalen didn't count. He might've been pissed

when he left after our fight, but he wouldn't have come after me like that. He wasn't that sort of man.

A little voice in my head whispered that I never would've thought my father was that sort of man either, but I ignored it. Even if I'd misjudged Jalen's character when it came to his willingness to commit violence, I couldn't see any scenario – even revenge – where he'd follow me, hit me over the head, then steal my purse. It would've been...pointless.

"Is there any reason why you think this wasn't some random mugging?" I asked. "My purse was taken off of me on the street. I wasn't assaulted. I mean, no more than what was needed to knock me down. It didn't happen at work or at home or even someplace like a bar or restaurant where I might've been followed. I was looking for a lost dog, and I'd only been hired an hour or so before."

The two men exchanged the sort of look that made me want to snap at them to stop treating me like a child, but I knew that what usually happened when a young woman told two adult men that she didn't want to be treated like a child, they did just that, even if they didn't seem to mean it.

Fortunately, I was saved from needing to find a way to get them to tell me what was going on when the door to the tiny room opened, and two more people walked in.

Clay was with a dark-haired man in his early fifties, a man I assumed was Agent Raymond Matthews. Considering that I'd never met the man before, the fact that he was here with Clay now told me that they were here on official business. I just didn't understand why.

"Since when are muggings under the FBI's jurisdiction?" I picked at the tape holding the medical gauze onto my palm.

"Detectives, thank you for getting Miss Quick's statement," Agent Matthews said gruffly. "Unless we find evidence to support a connection, we won't be interfering in your investigation, but you're welcome to ask for our assistance."

A connection? What the hell did *that* mean?

"We'll be in touch, Miss Quick," the older detective said, "if any of your property is found or if we need your help with identification."

I doubted either of those scenarios was likely, but I nodded anyway. As soon as the door closed behind the younger detective, I turned back to Clay and Agent Matthews.

"All right, what are you two doing here?" I pointed at Clay. "And don't give me some bullshit about wanting to make sure I was okay. Checking in on me doesn't require your partner to come with you, no matter how much you'd argue to the contrary."

Agent Matthews cracked a smile. "She knows you well."

"You're right," Clay said to me, his expression still somber. "I'm not here as a friend. Or, at least, not *only* as a friend. It's business, and not anything to do with getting mugged. Probably."

My insides squirmed. "What's going on? Stop beating around the bush and just tell me."

Clay looked at his partner who nodded. "There's no

easy way to say this, Rona, so I'm just going to come out with it."

I braced myself, but nothing could have truly prepared me for what came out of his mouth next.

"Your father's escaped."

THIRTY

I HAD TO HAVE MISHEARD WHAT CLAY SAID BECAUSE there was no way my father had escaped from prison only a month after he'd been found guilty of murder for a second time. They couldn't have been stupid enough to give a man like him the opportunity to escape. It had to be a mistake. A joke. A very unfunny joke.

I blinked slowly, wondering if maybe I was hearing things. I *had* gotten hit hard on the head today. That was a good possibility. I was going to go with the concussion as the reason I'd heard that absolute insanity.

"Rona, did you hear me?" Clay crossed over to where I was standing. He reached out as if he wanted to touch me, but then dropped his hand when he remembered that his partner was standing next to him.

I nodded. "I heard you, but I don't see how that's possible." I was surprised at how calm I sounded.

It was Agent Matthews who explained things. More or less. "A little under two hours ago, we received a call from

Indiana State Prison saying that your father escaped their custody."

Okay, that was definitely less rather than more.

As my head cleared, I knew I had to accept that what they were saying was true, but I wasn't going to be satisfied with such a simple explanation. "Again, I don't see how that's possible." I crossed my arms, winced, then scowled. "What happened?"

"I'm afraid we can't discuss an ongoing investigation," Agent Matthews said. "Especially since there are multiple agencies involved."

"Like hell you can't," I snapped. "My *father* broke out of *prison*. The same convicted murderer I had to testify against for the *second* time. The same man who tried to kill me. Who *almost* killed me." A thought suddenly hit me, and I slid off the bed, needing to stand even if my legs gave out on me. "For all I know, he tried to kill me again tonight."

"That's not possible," Agent Matthews said. "Trust us, Willis Jacobe couldn't have been responsible for your mugging, even if that would've been something in his MO."

"His *MO*?" I snapped at the agent. "His *MO* is to butcher people with the sharpest object he can find, but I'm pretty sure he wouldn't have minded using a rock if he thought it'd get the job done. I'm going to need something more than that as a reason to believe he didn't come after me again today."

Clay looked at Agent Matthews, who shook his head,

and then he turned back to me, a familiar stubborn set to his jaw.

"About an hour before you were mugged, Willis Jacobe was attacked by another inmate and both were taken to the infirmary. The prison doctor examined both inmates and sent the attacker back to his cell after bandaging up a few shallow cuts. Jacobe was admitted with multiple contusions and lacerations." Clay sounded like he'd swallowed a medical dictionary, but I was following what he was saying so I didn't protest. "The doctor was concerned about a blow to his head as he showed signs of being confused and disoriented, and with his history..."

I nodded, not needing him to finish that sentence. With my father's previous head injury, they'd want to be careful, especially since the prior injury had caused his personality changes. The last thing they'd want would be him becoming someone else...again.

"So they kept him in the infirmary, and he got out from there?" I prompted.

"Basically," Clay said. "He'd been in there for about forty minutes when he started complaining of chest pain. When the doctor went over to administer a shot, Jacobe grabbed him and used the needle to get the keys to his cuffs."

"Brilliant. He didn't even pull some *Shawshank* sneaky escape. You guys let him get out right there in broad daylight." I had to admit, being pissed was infinitely better than worrying about who'd come after me, or what my father might do, or thinking about how much more I was going to hurt tomorrow.

"You do realize that the FBI doesn't have anything to do with the Indiana state penitentiary system, right?" Agent Matthews asked.

I glared at him. "I think Willis Jacobe is a dangerous murderer that the FBI, the state police – hell, every person whose job it is to serve and protect..." I blew out a long breath, then inhaled deeply, trying to slow my pounding pulse. "I made sure he got put away, but apparently, I was the only one doing whatever it took to keep people safe from him."

Despite his partner's presence, Clay did reach out this time and put his hand on my arm. "Jacobe kept the doctor hostage until he was able to grab a badge and use it to get out of prison. As near as anyone can figure, he snuck onto a laundry truck and vanished."

"But it wasn't early enough for him to have found me and hurt me." I went back to the original point.

"Correct," Agent Matthews said. "The local police are going to work on your mugging case, but Clay and I are here to make sure you're safe from your father."

"You two are going to keep me safe?" I gestured around me. "You do realize I'm in the hospital?"

"Because you were mugged," Clay said, "not because of your father."

I raised an eyebrow and ignored the pain as it stretched the cut on my forehead. "Really? That's what you're going with?"

He gave me a half-smiled to go with a half-shrug. "We told the US Marshals that we'd come talk to you about protective custody. That's all I want for you. To keep you safe." His expression sobered, and he reached out to squeeze my hand. "If not for you, let me do it for Anton."

I knew Clay meant well, but mentioning my uncle brought a memory rushing forward fast enough to make me stagger.

"How long have you been getting these threats?" I demanded as I tossed the envelope and letter onto the worn sofa.

My uncle glanced down for a moment before returning his attention to the salad he was making. "I don't always make friends in my profession, Rona."

His tone was mild, and he sounded so much like my mother that it sent a stab of pain through me. I usually tried to ignore how much he looked like her, but times like now made it hard, though not as much as when people commented on how much he and I looked alike since that reminded both of us of who we'd lost.

"I'm not a child, Uncle Anton," I said, glaring at him. "You should have told me that you were getting death threats."

He turned toward me and pushed his sleeves up higher on his arms. Most of my female classmates growing up – and a few of the guys – had swooned over my uncle's fore-arms and I'd often wondered if that was how things would've been if I'd had a brother.

"I have an entire filing cabinet full of letters like that," he said calmly. "I get them at least once or twice a week, though they usually come to the office and not here."

"Don't they scare you?" I asked. "Someone could hurt you."

I saw the shadow cross his face, and I knew that he'd understood what I was really scared of: that some crazy person would take him away from me like my father had taken my mother. He came over to where I was standing and pulled me to him in a hug. I tucked my head under his chin and let myself pretend that I was in junior high again, accepting comfort from my uncle because of some minor incident.

"'Courage is resistance to fear, mastery of fear, not absence of fear.'"

"Mark Twain." My words were muffled, but I knew he could hear them. "He also said something about school boards being idiots."

Uncle Anton laughed and took a step back. "That he did. And I happen to think that makes him more credible."

I managed a smile. "Are you sure it's safe for you to go to court tomorrow?"

"Nothing's ever one hundred percent safe," he said as he went back to his salad. "Cars and airplanes crash. Tornados and hurricanes happen. Random events, natural phenomenon, all of it is as likely as something malicious."

He hadn't answered my question. "Do you at least tell the police about the letters?"

"They know," he said. "And I have to let them do their job so I can do mine."

I'd let it go then. He'd seemed so calm, so in control. It wasn't until days later, after he'd been gunned down on the courthouse steps, after the case on his murder had been officially closed, that I'd learned the cops had tried to convince Clay to go into protective custody after the latest set of threats.

He'd turned them down, saying that he wasn't going to let someone scare him into silence.

I'd hated him for that.

It hadn't been until I'd started at Quantico that I'd started to understand why he'd done what he'd done, but as I stood in front of Clay and Agent Matthews, a similar offer hanging in the air between us, I realized that only now could I truly get it.

"Do you know the Mark Twain quote about courage?" I asked. I brushed my hair back from my face and squared my shoulders. "If I hide, my father accomplishes what he'd set out to do nearly ten years ago. I can't let the fear of him rule my life."

"Rona," Clay protested. "Be smart about this."

"Telling a woman that she's stupid isn't usually the best way to get her to listen."

A man's voice came from the doorway, but I didn't quite believe that I wasn't hearing things until my eyes confirmed what my ears heard.

Jalen.

I scowled at him. "What the fuck are you doing here?"

THIRTY-ONE

"I called him," Clay said as Jalen entered the room. "I knew you wouldn't accept protective custody, and I hoped he'd be able to talk you into it."

I shot Clay a glare before returning to glowering at Jalen. "You two are both on my shit list."

"I seem to have a permanent spot on it," Jalen said. He held up his hands in the universal 'I surrender' gesture. "Not that I don't deserve it."

"Since you two like to talk so much, you can talk to each other," I said. "I'm going home."

"No, you're not," Jalen said, then hurried to explain. "And that's not coming from me. I asked the doctor if you were ready to be discharged, and he said that you need to be kept overnight for observation because you got hit on the head."

I looked at Clay. "I can't believe you did this to me."

Clay stuck his hands in his pockets as Agent Matthews excused himself. "I would give you a choice and say that either Jalen stays with you or I put a uniform at your door, but you'll pick the cop just to spite him."

He wasn't wrong.

"So I'm not giving you a choice. You have to stay overnight, and with your father out there, you can't stay alone." Clay glanced through the doorway where he could see Agent Matthews talking with the doctor who'd examined me. "Talk things out with him, Rona. If he's still being an asshole, I'll take him up in the mountains and leave him there. But I think he might surprise you."

"Why are you defending him all of a sudden?" I asked sullenly. "Last I checked, you were on my side."

His expression softened. "I *am* on your side, Rona. But sometimes, you need someone to save you from yourself."

I could see how hard it was for Clay to tell me to try to work things out with Jalen, but he meant every word, and that more than anything convinced me to at least listen to what Jalen had to say. If nothing else, I'd at least get closure.

"All right," I said. "Jalen can stay, but when I kick him out after he says his bit, I'm not going to be calling you for a bodyguard. That's on you."

"Agreed," Clay said.

He took a step toward me, his hands starting to come out of his pockets before he seemed to think better of it and just smiled. It didn't quite reach his eyes, and my annoyance with him dimmed even more.

"If you need anything, just call me. The nurses have my work number and my personal one. If we hear anything about your mugger or your father, I'll let you know."

"Thanks," I said. I almost considered asking him to stay too, but I knew that would be selfish on my part, and I wasn't going to do that. Besides, I'd promised to give Jalen a chance to explain himself, and since I didn't know how personal that conversation would be, I didn't want to make things even more awkward between Clay and me.

He closed the door on the way out, leaving Jalen and me not just alone, but isolated. If I'd been at home, I'd have at least had the freedom to move around my apartment, keep my hands busy. Here, all I could do was get back into bed and hope that Jalen wasn't going to be as big of an ass as he had been that morning.

I wasn't feeling particularly optimistic about that.

"You wanted to talk," I said. "Talk."

"I – I mean – shit." He sighed. "I'm not good at this sort of thing."

"Apologizing or explaining?"

He rubbed his jaw, his stubble whispering as it scraped against his palm. He still looked like he hadn't shaved in a day or two, and his clothes were rumpled, but not in a 'genius forgot to sleep' way. Something had taken a toll on him over the last few days. I wanted to believe it was me, that missing me had affected him this way, but I couldn't let myself hope that was the case.

"I don't want to sound like I'm making excuses," he began, "but I want you to understand why I thought..." He shook his head. "No, before I get to the why, there's something you need to hear."

His eyes were blazing as he turned his gaze on me and

I was suddenly aware of how disheveled I looked. I hadn't even had the chance to wash the blood out of my hair.

"I was an idiot, and I'm sorry." Neither his voice nor his gaze wavered. "I jumped to conclusions. Again. I should have trusted you, and I should have talked to you. Both about how I was feeling this morning, and what made me go there."

"Thank you." I folded my arms more tightly around my middle. "And yes, you should have trusted me, but I already know why you went off. You told me about what Elise did to you."

A part of me wanted to tell him that was why it had hurt so much. He'd essentially held me responsible for something his ex had done. One bad relationship and that was how he measured women. I understood that what she'd done had been awful, but it wasn't like there was a series of betrayals and broken promises in his past.

Not like how I had losses piled up behind me, constant reminders of why I shouldn't let anyone close.

"It's more than that," he said. He glanced at me, then turned his face away, as if he couldn't quite bear to look at me as he spoke. "A part of me has even wondered if this is why I'd ended up with Elise in the first place."

I waited in silence, not wanting to influence his decision to talk to me. He had to choose me on his own. I couldn't accept anything less.

"My parents were never married." He began to pace as he spoke. "I never really thought much about it as a kid because a lot of my friends' parents weren't married either, or they had been married but had since divorced. My parents lived in the same house, and I had my dad's last name. We were a family, no matter what a piece of paper said. At least, that's what my dad always told me. It wasn't until I was older that I realized how sad my mom was whenever we talked about it."

I had one of those memory flashes that were like some sort of montage, bits and pieces all strung together, sometimes with a common theme. For me, the theme was 'bad marriage.' My parents had argued on and off in the years before the accident, so it wasn't like they'd had some sort of idyllic, fairytale life until the day everything changed, but it hadn't been the same sort of arguing that had come later. After the accident, the fights had turned ugly. Insults hurling through the air, shouted and screamed without any thought about who could hear. Things had been thrown and broken. Threats made.

I'd found my mom crying more than once, and she'd always told me it was okay, that Dad was just hurting, and he didn't mean any of it. She'd always encouraged me to remember him the way he was rather than what he'd become. Sometimes, I wondered if she'd still be alive if I'd pressed the issue, pointed out the dangers. If I'd only convinced her to leave.

"When I was eight, my dad left," Jalen continued. "I was sitting in our den, playing a video game, and he walked out with two suitcases. Never said goodbye. Never even looked back."

My heart broke for the boy he'd been, but there were plenty of men in solid, stable relationships who'd had similar childhoods. Like Jalen had said, his situation hadn't been unique.

"I only saw him a handful of times over the next two years, and whenever he was with me, he looked like he wished he was somewhere else. For my tenth birthday, I told my mom that I wanted to change my last name to her maiden name so we'd have the same last name. I had to ask my dad, and a part of me thought maybe this would be enough to get his attention. It wasn't. He signed the paperwork without blinking."

I held out my hand and Jalen came over to the bed. He gently wrapped his fingers around mine and sat next to me.

"It wasn't until I was older that I found out that my father had been cheating on my mother almost the entire time they'd been together. She'd known, and she hadn't done anything about it. She said it was because she'd been too scared of trying to make it on her own, but I think at least some of it was because she still loved him. Even after all that, she loved him." Jalen's thumb brushed back and forth across my knuckles, and I wondered if he was soothing himself as much as trying to soothe me. "He got married my senior year of high school, and I've heard he has a couple kids with his wife now. I don't know if she was one of the women he'd cheated on my mom with, or if he'd fallen in love with her later. I received a card when I graduated high school, and that was the last I've heard from him. I've never met his new wife or their kids."

"I'm sorry." I squeezed his fingers, not knowing what else to say or do. I felt bad for him, for what he'd gone through, but I didn't want to feel anything more than just the normal sympathy any decent human being would have. I couldn't feel those deeper things, not if he was going to keep breaking my heart.

Because that's what was happening every time he came at me with accusations. He was breaking my heart.

"It's not an excuse," he said. "I know that. There's no excuse for the way I've behaved. I just want you to see me...so maybe you can forgive me."

I could hear what he wasn't saying, that it wasn't just about forgiveness. He wanted us to be together again, or still, or whatever. To move past all of this by talking through things rather than trying to bury it. It was healthier that way, and I appreciated that he was trying to do this the right way.

I just wasn't sure if it was enough.

"I don't think she's ever stopped loving him. She has a new boyfriend. Not really new. They started dating two years ago, and she moved to Spain with him last year." He glanced over at me, but only for a moment, like he didn't dare to linger. Like it was dangerous to look too long. "The way my dad treated my mom destroyed her for a long time, and it fucked with my head more than I'd realized until recently. I never wanted to be in a position where I ended up like her. I didn't want to care so much that someone would be able to hurt me like that."

I swallowed hard, my heart skipping a beat when I realized the implications of what he was saying. I wouldn't put words in his mouth though. If he wanted me to know it, this, he'd have to say.

He raised my hand and kissed my knuckles, then

flipped it over, lightly tracing the bandage on my palm. His voice was soft. "I never thought it would be a problem. Even when Elise did what she did, it hurt, but I wasn't broken. I married her, and I thought I loved her. Maybe I did. Whatever I felt for her though, it wasn't strong enough for me to want to fight for her."

Was that what he was doing here? Fighting for me? Somehow, when I'd heard that phrase in the past, I'd always thought it would be something aggressive, something loud and in-your-face. But Jalen wasn't being any of those things. He was being vulnerable and honest.

And somehow, that felt more like fighting for me than anything my imagination would've come up with.

All of the feelings I'd tried to keep pushed down poked their heads up again. If he was as sincere as he sounded, I was in serious trouble. I could stand up against anger and accusations. I wasn't so sure I could hold up against *this* Jalen.

"I want to fight for you, Rona. For us." His grip on my hand tightened. "Please tell me that there's something to fight for."

I pulled my hand back. It was hard to think when he was touching me. "That sucks about your parents, but you can't keep holding others' actions against me. It's not fair."

"You're right," he agreed immediately. "I'm an asshole for doing it. And I'll never do it again. Please give me a second chance."

"I did."

His face flushed, but he didn't argue. "And I fucked it up, I know."

Here were the questions that mattered, no matter how much it hurt to ask them. "What makes this time different? Why should I trust you when you've proven you don't trust me?"

He slid off the bed and went to his knees. He was tall enough that he was still able to reach my hands. "I love you."

The words took my breath away.

"I know you have every right to be skeptical after what I've done, but I swear to you, if you let me, I will do whatever it takes to prove to you that I want this to work." He took my hands again. "You are the only person I've ever wanted a future with, Rona. The only person I can see. I love you, and I'm begging you to give me a chance to prove it."

THIRTY-TWO

It would've been smarter to have told him that there wasn't a chance, that he should leave and not speak to me again. It would hurt like hell, but better to hurt now than have my heart destroyed when he inevitably reverted back to being an asshole.

And he would.

Because I couldn't hope for anything else. It would only make things worse if I had my hopes up.

Still, I didn't have it in me to send him away.

Which was how we ended up with a tentative agreement where he'd stay with me in the hospital, and after I was released, we'd see where things stood.

I had to admit, it was more than a little amusing to see this big, rugged man playing nursemaid. Well, not really nursemaid, since it wasn't like I was bedridden. They just needed to keep an eye on my brain, and Jalen managed to convince the nurses and doctors that he could do that better by staying in the room with me than they could by waking me up every few hours to ask me my name.

He'd charmed them all, and I realized this was what he was like as a businessman. He might've been scary smart, but he also had to know how to interact with people to convince them to invest in his company or believe in what he was building. As I watched him smiling and talking to the doctors and nurses, I couldn't help but admire the easy confidence he exuded.

Then, I thought about how he was with me. How he had been when we'd first met versus the way he was now. He'd had that same brash impudence, almost arrogance, when we met for the first time. Hell, we'd been in the middle of an argument when he'd kissed me, and he hadn't seemed the slightest bit concerned that I might not want him. He'd always known exactly what he'd wanted and gone after it.

But now, he hesitated around me, calculating each touch, each word. He wasn't timid, but he'd lost the self-assurance he'd once had regarding my feelings for him.

Attraction and emotions weren't the problem though. I still wanted him. I still cared about him. Maybe more than cared, if I allowed myself to go there. Trust was the issue. I wasn't holding a grudge about the things he'd said. I'd forgiven him for all that. But I didn't trust him to not do it again.

Those were the things I kept telling myself as the hours past, and he worked to prove himself to me. Anything I wanted or needed, he got it, whether it was something to read or help with my pillows. It would've been annoying if I hadn't been able to see how much it meant to him.

We were in the middle of a debate about the merits of rebooting television and movie series when I dozed off. A nurse woke me a couple hours later when she came in to check on me.

She smiled at me, and it took me a moment to realize she wasn't just being friendly. Jalen had fallen asleep too, his head resting on his arm, both of which were on the edge of my bed. His other hand was next to mine, our fingers lightly entwined, and I instinctively knew that I'd been the one to reach for him.

"You have quite a young man there, Miss Quick." She kept her voice low as she checked my vitals. "He really loves you."

"He does, doesn't he?" I murmured. I reached across my body to brush hair back from his forehead. Even with the scruff on his face, he looked younger in his sleep, and I couldn't help remembering what he'd told me about his childhood.

"Everything's looking good," the nurse said, drawing my attention back to her. "Barring any changes, you should be cleared to be discharged in the morning. The doctor will have to double-check everything and sign off on it, but it should all be routine."

"That's good news," I said with a distracted smile.

I was glad for the news, but I couldn't deny the lump in my stomach when I thought about leaving. Jalen had been great with all this, but I'd suddenly realized that he'd proven before that he was great in these sorts of situations. He'd been wonderful when Adare had been in the hospital and even after she died. Great when he'd shown up in Indiana during my father's trial. When he got to play the white knight, he excelled. It was the every day that seemed to throw him.

I supposed we'd see how things went later today when it was time for me to leave. With that thought on my mind, I tried to fall back asleep, knowing that nothing I did would make things more restful for me. I wouldn't really get to do that until I was back in my own bed.

―――――

"I THINK you should come home with me," Jalen announced as we waited for the doctor to sign off on my discharge paperwork.

"Why's that?" I asked as I fidgeted with the hem of the shirt I was wearing.

Jalen had run out first thing this morning and bought clothes for me to wear home. Since he'd only gone to the dollar store one block over, he'd chosen for practicality rather than fashion, and they would've been great if I'd been able to put them on after a shower. Yet another reason why I couldn't wait to get out of here.

"Even if the mugging was random, the thief has your driver's license, which means he knows where you live."

Shit. I hadn't even thought about that. I canceled my credit cards yesterday – thankfully, I'd had my phone in my pants pocket rather than my purse when I'd been attacked – but I hadn't thought about the information my driver's license would give him.

"Then there's your father," Jalen continued. "We both know Clay wouldn't want you being alone until your dad's found."

He had another good point.

Dammit.

"What Clay doesn't know won't hurt him?" I made it a question.

Jalen shook his head. "Sorry. On this one, Clay and I see eye-to-eye. My house has a top-grade security system. You'll be safe with me."

Physically, yes, I'd be safe. I wasn't so sure about how my heart would come out of this. Still, the thought of going home now that I was aware of the danger that could be waiting, my options were limited.

"All right," I agreed. "We'll go to your house for now, and I'll figure out where to go from there."

He didn't look thrilled at the mention of me finding somewhere else to stay, but he didn't try to talk me into anything else. I knew he'd probably bring it up at another time, but that was a worry for later.

Less than ninety minutes later, we were pulling up to his house. It had started snowing at some point in time this morning, thick, wet flakes that stuck to everything, including the roads. If it kept up like this, I'd have the chance to see just how good the snow tires on my car worked. I hadn't driven much in snow despite the fact that I'd lived up north most of my life. Obviously, I'd been too young in Indiana, and since I'd lived my teenage years in

New York City, I hadn't even gotten my license until I graduated.

"Careful," Jalen said as he opened my door and held out a hand. "The garage is heated most of the time, but the heating system for it went on the fritz a couple days ago, and I'm waiting for someone to come out and fix it."

I wondered if he knew how much it said about his character that he was willing to wait for a repairman rather than offering to pay for preferential treatment.

I took his hand, a little thrill of electricity going through me as our skin made contact. My joints were stiff, and the places where bruises had bloomed ached as I let him help me from the car. The thing about having a serrated kitchen knife dragged through your flesh, other pain is mild by comparison. Still, it didn't stop me from grimacing as Jalen led me into the house.

"Are you hungry?" he asked as we paused in the kitchen.

I shook my head. "I'd really like a shower and clean clothes. How long do you think I should stay here?"

"Until Clay says you're safe."

I scowled at him. "The two of you ganging up on me isn't fair."

One corner of Jalen's mouth tipped up in a partial smile. "Yes, well, protecting you is one thing we can agree on."

"So I'm just supposed to wait who knows how long to clean up?"

"No," he said, moving me forward again. "You're supposed to accept my offer of the use of my home. I have a guest bedroom and bathroom where you can clean up and rest."

"And my clothes? I don't think you have any of those lying around."

He ignored my sarcasm and answered my question seriously. "My clothes will work just fine. They'll be big, but it's not like you'll be going much of anywhere. Clay's supposed to check in tomorrow. I'll ask him then if it's safe for me to take you back to your place so you can get a few things."

"Fine," I said, too tired to argue.

It wasn't as much a physical tired as it was an emotional one. I planned on taking as long as possible in the shower so I could finally have a break from Jalen. I appreciated everything he'd done for me, but without any time alone, I hadn't been able to really think about all the things he'd said to me.

When I stepped under the spray, I sighed with relief. The heat felt good against my sore muscles, and the sound chased away the chaotic thoughts I hadn't been able to banish. I stood there for what seemed like hours before I even started washing up, just letting my mind go blank. By the time I reached for the shampoo, I was ready to do some serious soul-searching about everything Jalen had said. He deserved an honest answer about whether or not we could get past this.

He was sitting on the guest room bed when I emerged from the bathroom, a billow of steam accompanying me. I'd changed into the clothes he'd given me, and they were far from revealing, but the fact that I hadn't had a clean bra or underwear with me meant that beneath the soft cotton t-shirt and cuffed sweatpants, I was naked. I crossed my arms over my chest, hoping he couldn't tell that my nipples were hard. It was from the temperature difference. Nothing else. Certainly not because of the heat I saw on his face.

"I was starting to get worried," he said as he stood. "I thought you might've passed out in there and I'd have to rush you back to the hospital."

"Just thinking," I said. "And enjoying being clean again."

"Thinking about what?" His tone was casual, but I saw the tension in his body.

"About how I feel," I admitted. "About you, about all the things you said, about whether or not I could trust you again."

He turned away from me, hiding whatever expression he couldn't keep off his face. "Make it a clean break," he said quietly. "That's all I ask."

"It will take a while to build that trust again," I said, closing the distance between us. I put my hand on his back, and he stiffened. "But what you said made me face something I've been struggling with. You're not just another guy, J. You're not replaceable." I took a deep breath and made my own confession. "I love you too."

THIRTY-THREE

THE SILENCE THAT FOLLOWED MY STATEMENT WAS thick and heavy with all the possibilities that came with my admission. I dropped my hand and whatever paralysis had held him in place snapped. He spun around and took my face between his hands, his expression hot and searching, desperate.

"Do you mean it?" he asked, his voice low. "It's okay if you don't, if you thought you should say it just because I did–"

I put my fingers on his lips. "I meant it. I *mean* it. I want to fight for us, see whatever this is between us can become." I put my hand on his chest and felt the steady beat of his heart against my palm. "I want this to become something."

His mouth came down on mine, softer, gentler than it had ever been before. A hand slid up into my wet hair, tangling in the locks that nearly brushed my shoulders. I waited for the pull, the pain against my scalp, and anticipation pooled in my belly, hot liquid arousal. It didn't come. His touch remained tender.

I slid my hands under his shirt, and his muscles jumped under my fingers. I scraped my teeth across his bottom lip, bit it, and he moaned. His grip tightened, just a little, but I could feel it now, all the strength that he was holding back, all the power in that strong, muscular body of his, waiting to be released.

"I want you." He breathed the words against my skin as his mouth moved to the side of my mouth, to my jaw. "Damn, Rona, I want you so much."

"Then take me." I tucked my fingers into the waistband of his jeans and pulled him tighter against me. "I've missed you."

He groaned, his forehead resting against mine. "Do you have any idea how fucking hard it is to resist you?"

"Then don't."

"I have to," he insisted, his eyes scanning my features. "You're hurt."

I laughed softly. "I was hurt the first time we had sex, if you remember."

"I remember," he said, his voice low and husky. "I remember how it felt, being inside you that first time. How it was like being...home."

I closed my eyes and whispered, "It was like that for me too."

His laugh vibrated through me. "You're really not making this easy for me."

"Good." I slid my hands around to his ass and dug my nails in. "Because I want it to be *hard*."

He leaned back as he laughed again, louder this time. "Seriously? You're making sex puns?"

I shrugged and grinned at him. "It seemed appropriate."

He wrapped his arms around me, resting his hands at the small of my back. "You should get some sleep."

"It's three o'clock in the afternoon," I said. "I don't want to sleep. Do you want to sleep?"

"I told you what I want," he said, his expression sobering. "But it doesn't change the fact that you're hurt."

"It's too bad," I said as I took a step back. I smiled up at him as I reached down to grab the bottom of his shirt. "Because that means I'll just have to lay down on that nice comfy bed and make myself feel better."

His eyes went dark, the sort of dark that twisted things inside me. "And how, exactly, are you planning to do that?"

I wet my bottom lip, even more aware than before of what I wasn't wearing under his clothes. "Do you want details?" I smiled as I stepped back until my legs bumped against the bed. "Like how I'd take off my shirt and run my hands over my breasts? How I'd play with my nipples until they're tight and aching. Slide my hand under these sweats and rub my fingers over my clit, feel how wet I am—"

Everything else I'd planned on saying was cut off when Jalen buried his hands in my hair and his mouth crashed into mine. The hesitation was gone, replaced by the same desperate need I felt clawing at my insides.

Our clothes hit the floor as we scrambled out of them, forgotten the moment they left our hands. His skin was hot, hands burning paths across my limbs, my torso. I gasped, back arching as his lips wrapped around my nipple.

"That feels amazing," I moaned, closing my eyes.

Every pull of his mouth went straight to my clit, and I writhed under the heavy weight of his body. Skin and muscle, friction and pressure. Our bodies moved against each other, slick and sweet, a dance that we'd known from the first moment we'd come together.

He worked his way up to my collarbone, sucking and biting as he murmured words, endearments. Some of them I could make out, some I couldn't, but it didn't matter. I knew how he felt, I could feel how much he wanted me. His fingers played over my ribcage, then he palmed my hip, my ass, and then pulled my leg up and around his waist.

He raised his head, his eyes locking with mine. The depth of what I saw there took my breath away, and then he was sliding into me.

Home.

He'd chosen the right word when he described what it was like when the two of us came together. It was home. *He* was home.

The idea should have terrified me, but as he rocked against me, I couldn't feel anything but the warmth of the feelings we'd confessed, the pleasure of how our bodies came together.

"J, J," I whimpered. "I need more. Harder, please. More."

"I've got you," he said. He lowered his head and brushed his lips across mine. "I've got you, Rona, and I'm not going to lose you again."

I reached up and wrapped my hand around the back of his neck, pulling him down for another kiss. Our tongues tangled together as he sat up, taking me with him. The new position changed the way we fit together, putting new and intense pressure on all sorts of wonderful places. Then his finger slid lower, between my cheeks, and I tore my mouth from his, cursing as he rubbed over that tight ring of muscle.

"Do you want my finger in there?" he asked as he fisted my hair, pulling my head back. "Will you come if my finger's in your ass? Will that make you come, baby?"

My nails raked across his shoulders, hard enough to make him hiss, and his cock swelled even more inside me. His hips jerked upward, driving into me with the exact right amount of force to push me toward climax. Then the tip of his finger breached my ass, and I shattered. He followed a moment later, my name a strangled cry.

Before the strength returned to my legs, Jalen was up and in the bathroom. He returned with a washcloth and cleaned me up, not enough that I wouldn't need another shower, but enough that I could relax for a bit.

Even though I'd felt that things with us were better, different, I was a bit surprised when he climbed back into bed and pulled us both under the covers. He reached out to me, pulling me close. I smiled at the way we still fit together, even when our bodies were no longer joined.

"Is it just me, or does this feel...right?" Jalen asked as he kissed the top of my head.

"It does," I said, running my fingers over the arm

around my waist. "We're still going to have to work at things, you know?"

"I know." He paused for a moment, then continued, "Do you remember the blindfold we used before?"

I looked over my shoulder at him. "Yes?"

The memory still made me flush.

His expression was serious as he reached up and ran his thumb across my bottom lip. "I want you to use it on me."

He didn't look away as I stared at him, wondering if I understood him correctly. Being blindfolded required trust, handing over control, and that was what he was offering me. His trust, his control.

Whatever I might have said was lost as the front door slammed open.

"Jalen! Where the hell are you?!"

THIRTY-FOUR

Of course, Elise would have to come in and ruin everything. I really despised that woman.

As I scrambled out of bed to grab my discarded clothes, Jalen did the same.

"Don't you think it's time to take away her key?" I asked. The question was serious but didn't have any bite to it. One look at his face was all the confirmation I needed that he didn't want Elise here any more than I did.

"I did," Jalen said. "She must've had another one...or we didn't lock the door when we came in."

I'd barely gotten the pants back on when I heard footsteps on the stairs. I glanced toward the bathroom, wondering if I could hide in there until she was gone, but time wasn't on my side. Besides, it wasn't like I'd done anything wrong. The only reason Jalen and Elise weren't divorced was because she refused to sign the papers. From what I knew of her, I suspected it had less to do with real feelings for Jalen and more to do with the 'perks' that came with being married to a handsome, wealthy man.

"Jalen!"

"I'll be right down!" he shouted back. He shot me a helpless look. "I'm sorry about this."

I shook my head and mustered a smile. "It's not your fault."

I meant the words too, but it didn't mean I wasn't frustrated. I'd had a rough few days, and now that things were on the mend between us, the idea of hiding here with Jalen for a little while was more appealing than I wanted to admit.

The door slammed open, and I straightened, refusing to be embarrassed. I had nothing to be ashamed of; neither of us did. It didn't stop the flush from creeping up my cheeks, but that could be explained as easily by arousal and physical exertion.

"What are you doing in here?" Elise demanded. Her eyes flicked over to me for the briefest of moments, and then her attention was back on Jalen. "It doesn't matter. We need to talk."

"You can't keep coming in here like this, Elise," Jalen said. "When I told you to give back your key, I didn't mean that you could use another one."

"I didn't have to," she said, giving him a simpering smile. "The door was unlocked. You should really be more careful. *Anyone* could let themselves in."

Subtle.

"I've already told you that we're not talking about anything without our lawyers present," Jalen said. He moved closer to me, angling his body so that he was between Elise and me. "You need to leave and call your attorney. He'll call mine, and we'll set up a meeting. If you're not here about the divorce, then I don't want to hear it."

She crossed her arms and smirked. "Oh, you'll want to hear what I have to say." She gestured to me. "But you probably won't want *her* to hear it."

I stepped up to Jalen's side and put my hand on his arm. "I'll leave if he asks me to, but he knows I'm here for him, no matter what you say."

She looked at Jalen, an expectant expression on her face. When he didn't say anything, her mouth twisted into a scowl. "Let's test that theory."

She stepped into the bedroom, coming close enough to touch. Jalen reached down and took my hand, threading his fingers between mine. Her eyes narrowed, but it didn't stop her.

"Remember that night when we got together to talk about the divorce? Without the lawyers. We ordered in and opened a bottle of wine."

Jalen stiffened, and I knew whatever was coming wouldn't be easy to hear, but I wasn't going to jump to conclusions. If we were going to trust each other, it had to begin somewhere.

"Well, sweetie, I don't know how else to say it, but I'm pregnant. You're going to be a father."

She beamed at him while my stomach dropped. I wasn't going to jump to conclusions. I needed to give him a chance to refute what she was saying, and I kept reminding myself of that as I tried not to look like I wanted to throw up.

"That was more than two months ago." Jalen's voice was strained. "You would've known before now."

My hand tightened around his. They'd had sex more recently than I'd thought. Okay, I could handle that. Like he said, it'd been more than two months ago. Before he and I had even met. Hell, I'd slept with Clay less than a week before I met Jalen. If he wasn't going to hold that against me, it'd be hypocritical of me to be upset about him having sex with his wife.

"Things have just been so stressful lately, you know." Elise reached into her purse and pulled out a folded piece of paper. "What with you wanting to divorce me and all. I thought that was why I'd been so tired and not wanting to eat, but my doctor ran some blood work just in case, and he called me yesterday with the results."

I went numb. Elise was pregnant. Jalen was going to be a father.

"I want a paternity test," Jalen said, his voice cold.

I pulled my hand away. He didn't believe he was the father. My father had accused my mother of the same thing. Everyone said that was why he'd killed her. She'd cheated on him and gotten pregnant. At least, that was what he'd believed. The DNA test after autopsy had proven his accusations false.

"Jalen, how could you ask that?" Elise sniffed, her bottom lip trembling.

"Are you serious, Elise? How can I ask that? You cheated on me. I have no idea who you've slept with in the time we were separated. Hell, I don't even know who you were fucking when we were still together. I can't believe anything you say without actual proof."

A flare of anger went through me at his accusation, but rational thought quickly followed. He wasn't making baseless accusations. He'd literally walked in on her having sex with another man. It wasn't something he made up, assumed, or even took out of context. Over the years they'd been together, she'd proven more than once that she couldn't be trusted.

"A paternity test this early could hurt the baby." She put her hands on her still-flat stomach. "I couldn't do that to our child." She sniffled again. "But if you feel like you have to know right now..."

"I want to talk to a doctor to find out when it's safe to do one," Jalen said.

I didn't want to be here. This wasn't a conversation I should be involved in.

"Of course," Elise said, giving him a watery smile. "I asked the doctor about all the things we'd need to do." She unfolded the paper she'd taken out of her purse. "I have a list of all of our doctor's appointments. Then there's the prenatal vitamins and special diet I need to be on. I've already talked to my agent, and she said she'll start setting up maternity shoots for me so I can work until closer to my due date."

Jalen was starting to look overwhelmed, and I couldn't blame him. He'd gone from thinking she was completely out of his life to being bound to her forever if he wanted a relationship with his child.

"I'm thinking the two-bedroom suite will be perfect for a nursery and a live-in nanny."

That was it. I couldn't stand here and listen to her talk about all the ways she'd be worming her way back into Jalen's life. I couldn't argue with her either, not without sounding like some selfish bitch who was only concerned about how things affected me.

I headed for the door, trying to leave as quietly and quickly as possible. I half-expected Elise to stop me, force me to listen to everything, but she didn't even pause as I stepped behind her and out the door. I practically ran down the steps, shoving my shoes onto my feet, and grabbing my coat before running out into the snow.

THIRTY-FIVE

I WAS HALF-WAY DOWN THE DRIVEWAY WHEN I HEARD Jalen yelling my name. I frantically brushed at my cheeks, not wanting him to see me cry and take it the wrong way. I ducked my head and kept going, pretending that I didn't hear him begging me to stop.

Then his hand latched onto my arm, and he spun me around. His expression was stricken, and it cut me to the bone, adding to the pain already growing in my chest.

"I didn't cheat on you, Rona. I swear it." He reached up to push my hair out of my eyes. "I love you, and I have my faults, but I'd never cheat on you."

"I know." I leaned into the hand he put on my cheek. "And I'm not angry at you. I still trust you, and I love you."

A shadow crossed his face. "But?"

I reluctantly took a step back. "But you can't abandon your child."

"I can't," he agreed. His hands opened and closed like he wanted to reach for me again but kept stopping himself.

"That makes me love you even more." My voice quavered, and I took a slow breath. "But even though it doesn't change how I feel, it changes things between us."

"It doesn't have to," he said. "Please, Rona."

I gave him the best smile I could, but I knew it wasn't even close to enough. "Having a baby changes things. From a practical standpoint, if nothing else. You need to be there for Elise. The two of you have to figure out how this changes things between you. How you'll parent. Where you'll live. It's a lot."

"I don't want to lose you."

I swallowed hard, fighting back a fresh wave of tears. "I'm not breaking up with you, not unless it's what you want, but you need time and space to decide how your life will look with this new addition to it. And I need time and space to process it too."

"Rona." He took a step toward me, and I held up a hand. "It's not safe for you to be alone. You should stay."

A shiver ran up my spine as I remembered that my father had escaped. I was here under Jalen's protection, or should be.

But I needed to go.

I shook my head. "I'll go straight home and lock up," I promised. "You need to go back inside. When we're both ready, we'll talk." I turned away and focused on putting one foot in front of the other. I'd call for a cab before I reached his gate, then wait inside the safety of those bars until it arrived. It would be okay. Right now, it was more important to get away.

He called after me again, but I didn't slow this time,

and he didn't chase me. As much as a part of me wished he had, I knew this was for the best. We might be able to get through it, after all. This wasn't broken trust or loss of love. It'd have its own set of problems, but nothing the two of us couldn't manage. We'd gotten through worse.

These were all the things I told myself over and over as I trudged through the snow to the gate. I didn't know how much time passed before I heard an approaching car, but I was glad for it. I'd used a new app to call for a ride, and they'd gotten here quicker than I'd expected. I ran through the side gate and waited for it to pull up next to me.

When it stopped, I frowned and pulled out my phone to double check my memory. The app had said my car would be a tan Subaru. I didn't know a lot about cars, but this definitely wasn't a Subaru. And it wasn't tan. It was an SUV, and it was dark blue, almost black.

Alarm bells started going off in my head, but not fast enough. A man jumped out of the passenger's side seat and grabbed me, pinning my arms at my sides. My phone fell on the ground, and he kicked it away. I struggled, putting everything I had into trying to break free.

Then his hand was on my face, a cloth covering my mouth and nose. The sickly-sweet smell I knew to be chloroform invaded my senses, and I tried to scream.

One beat.

Two beats.

My heart echoed in my ears, slowing from its previous frantic pace. My limbs felt heavy, and my eyes closed.

One beat.

Two beats.

Everything went dark and my thoughts faded.
Gone.

THE END

The New Pleasures series continues in the final book, *Saved by Him*.

Indecent Encounter

Dom X Box Set

Unlawful Attraction Box Set

Chasing Perfection Box Set

Blindfold Box Set

Club Prive Box Set

The Pleasure Series Box Set

Exotic Desires Box Set

Casual Encounter Box Set

Sinful Desires Box Set

Twisted Affair Box Set

Serving HIM Box Set

Pure Lust Box Set

ABOUT THE AUTHOR

M. S. Parker is a USA Today Bestselling author and the author of over fifty spicy romance series and novels.

Living part-time in Las Vegas, part-time on Maui, she enjoys sitting by the pool with her laptop writing her next spicy romance.

Growing up all she wanted to be was a dancer, actor and author. So far only the latter has come true but M. S. Parker hasn't retired her dancing shoes just yet. She is still waiting for the call to appear on Dancing With The Stars.

When M. S. isn't writing, she can usually be found reading– oops, scratch that! She is always writing.

For more information:
www.msparker.com
msparkerbooks@gmail.com

ACKNOWLEDGMENTS

First, I would like to thank all of my readers. Without you, my books would not exist. I truly appreciate each and every one of you.

A big THANK YOU goes out to all the Facebook fans, street team, beta readers, and advanced reviewers. You are a HUGE part of the success of all my series.

Also thank you to my editor Lynette, my proofreader Nancy, and my wonderful cover designer, Sinisa. You make my ideas and writing look so good.

Made in the USA
Middletown, DE
04 March 2021

34806323R00146